He stared at the tiny s ... *his hand...*

...and pictured Kenna wearing nothing more than the soft lace—an image that was arousing and unnerving.

Daniel was intimately acquainted with women's lingerie. He knew the difference between a G-string and a thong, appreciated the effect of a push-up bra.

He wouldn't mind seeing what Kenna looked like in one...and then out of it.

"Stay out of my underwear drawer."

He looked at Kenna and grinned. "I never gave much thought to getting into it...until a moment ago."

"Well, stop. Just because I'm your wife doesn't mean I'm going to get naked with you. You set the terms," she reminded him. "A one-year marriage on paper only."

Obviously not a well thought-out plan, he realized.

"What if I want to renegotiate?" he asked.

"Not going to happen."

He took a step closer, deliberately invading her personal space. "You know I can't resist a challenge."

* * *

THOSE ENGAGING GARRETTS!:
The Carolina Cousins

Dear Reader,

Welcome back to Charisma, North Carolina.

Daniel Garrett and Kenna Scott first appeared in *The Single Dad's Second Chance* (June 2014). In that story, it was revealed that twenty-seven-year-old Daniel was trying to access the money his maternal grandfather had tied up in trust until he attained the age of thirty—or was legally married.

Of course, Daniel has no intention of getting married just to get his hands on the funds...unless he can get his hands on his gal pal at the same time. Kenna doesn't have any plans to marry for love *or* money...but then her best friend presents her with an irresistible proposal.

I've always enjoyed stories where the friendship between a man and a woman proves to be not the defining characteristic of their relationship but the foundation of something more, and I had a lot of fun watching Daniel and Kenna realize exactly that. I hope you enjoy their story.

Happy reading,

Brenda Harlen

PS. If you want to read more of the Those Engaging Garretts! series, watch for Nathan's story, coming in spring 2015.

A Wife for One Year

—

Brenda Harlen

HARLEQUIN® SPECIAL EDITION®

If you purchased this book without a cover you should be aware that this book is stolen property. It was reported as "unsold and destroyed" to the publisher, and neither the author nor the publisher has received any payment for this "stripped book."

Recycling programs
for this product may
not exist in your area.

ISBN-13: 978-0-373-65830-5

A WIFE FOR ONE YEAR

Copyright © 2014 by Brenda Harlen

All rights reserved. Except for use in any review, the reproduction or utilization of this work in whole or in part in any form by any electronic, mechanical or other means, now known or hereinafter invented, including xerography, photocopying and recording, or in any information storage or retrieval system, is forbidden without the written permission of the publisher, Harlequin Enterprises Limited, 225 Duncan Mill Road, Don Mills, Ontario M3B 3K9, Canada.

This is a work of fiction. Names, characters, places and incidents are either the product of the author's imagination or are used fictitiously, and any resemblance to actual persons, living or dead, business establishments, events or locales is entirely coincidental.

This edition published by arrangement with Harlequin Books S.A.

For questions and comments about the quality of this book, please contact us at CustomerService@Harlequin.com.

® and TM are trademarks of Harlequin Enterprises Limited or its corporate affiliates. Trademarks indicated with ® are registered in the United States Patent and Trademark Office, the Canadian Intellectual Property Office and in other countries.

HARLEQUIN

TM www.Harlequin.com

Printed in U.S.A.

BRENDA HARLEN

is a former family law attorney turned work-at-home mom and national bestselling author who has written more than twenty books for Harlequin. Her work has been validated by industry awards (including an RWA Golden Heart Award and the *RT Book Reviews* Reviewers' Choice Award) and by the fact that her kids think it's cool that she's "a real author."

Brenda lives in southern Ontario with her husband and two sons. When she isn't at the computer working on her next book, she can probably be found at the arena, watching a hockey game. Keep up to date with Brenda on Facebook, follow her on Twitter, at @BrendaHarlen, or send her an email at brendaharlen@yahoo.com.

To my husband of twenty years:

Thanks for all of your love, support and encouragement over the past two decades—and especially for your patience and understanding when other (fictional!) men become the focus of my attention as I work toward deadlines...

Prologue

Life was all about trade-offs, Kenna Scott realized as she made her way through the corridors of Hillfield Academy, the private school she'd transferred to three weeks earlier. Her high marks had won her a scholarship to the prestigious school, but her secondhand uniform, scuffed shoes and ancient backpack still marked her as a "charity case" to her fellow students.

There was no hiding the fact that she was from the wrong part of town, where she lived in the erroneously named "Royal Towers"—a three-story apartment building with rusted balconies, cracked sidewalks and a landlord who sold dime bags in the back of the parking lot. Even working two jobs, it was the best her mother could provide for them, and putting food on the table for three kids without a penny from any of their good-for-nothing fathers wasn't easy.

So Kenna didn't expect anything to come easy for her, either, but it was harder than she'd thought it would be to ignore the snarky whispers and the disdainful glances of the other kids at Hillfield. Thankfully, they gave her a wide berth, as if her lower-class status might somehow be infectious.

All of them except Daniel Garrett.

At her other school, labs had been assigned alphabetically. But for some reason, Mr. Taylor liked to mix things up—test the randomness of chemistry, he explained. Basically he put names in a hat and pulled two out together, and those two would be lab partners for the duration of the semester. That was how she ended up with Daniel Garrett as her lab partner in junior year.

Which she didn't really mind, because he wasn't a complete goof-off like some of the other kids. Although he focused on the work they had to do, he was always asking her questions, about what books she liked to read or the kind of movies she liked to watch.

Finally, on the Friday of the third week of class and after the latest round of questioning, she asked, "What's with the interrogation?"

"I'm trying to get to know you."

"Just because we're lab partners doesn't mean we have to be friends."

"It doesn't have to keep us from being friends, either," Daniel pointed out.

"And even if we were friends, it wouldn't get you into my pants."

"Excuse me?"

"You think I didn't see you and your friends in the cafeteria, looking at me and snickering, probably making bets on how easy I am because I'm from South Ridge and here on a scholarship?"

He held up his hands in mock surrender. "Okay, there was some talk," he admitted. "Not because you're a scholarship student from South Ridge but because you're hot. And yeah, some of the guys bet that I couldn't get you to go out with me, so I thought I'd give it a shot."

She hadn't expected him to admit it. And she hadn't anticipated that a casual comment on her appearance would make her stomach feel all quivery inside. She'd often been told that she was beautiful—usually by male "friends" of her mother—and those remarks had always made her uncomfortable. As a result, she'd dressed to hide her feminine curves and downplay her appearance, but the uniform requirements at Hillfield didn't allow her to cover up with baggy jeans or oversize sweaters.

But the matter-of-fact tone of Daniel's statement didn't make her uneasy, and the way he looked at her didn't make her wary. So she summoned the courage to ask, "How much?"

"What?"

"How much was the wager?"

He shifted uncomfortably. "A hundred bucks."

She didn't react, wouldn't let him see how much that kind of money would mean to her. Even half of it was a fortune to her, and these guys threw it around on a lame-ass bet without a second thought.

After a few minutes, she said, "We could split it."

"What?"

She almost smiled at this proof she'd surprised him. "If you give me half and buy the pizza out of your fifty, I'll let you win that bet."

He seemed to consider her offer for a minute, then nodded and held out his hand. "Deal."

She felt an unexpected jolt when her palm made contact with his, but she refused to acknowledge it. She wasn't interested in any chemistry outside of this classroom.

Chapter One

Ten years later

Kenna Scott owed Daniel Garrett more than she could ever possibly repay him.

Not that he would agree. The first time he'd ever bailed her out of a difficult situation, he'd told her, "Friends don't keep score." And while she hadn't really kept score over the years, it was an undeniable truth that he'd come to her rescue more times than she wanted to admit. Now she was in the unique position of being able to help him.

Twenty-four hours earlier, she wouldn't have imagined there was anything he could ask of her that she would refuse.

Twenty-four hours earlier, she wouldn't have imagined he'd ask her to marry him.

As their taxi zipped through the streets of Las Vegas, her feelings were as much a blur as the scenery outside the window.

Was she really going to go through with this? Was she going to marry Daniel to help him gain access to the trust fund that was tied up until his thirtieth birthday or he was "lawfully married"?

And was a marriage under such circumstances considered lawful?

"You're having second thoughts," he guessed.

She looked at him—the man who had been one of her best friends for the past decade—and felt a little flutter of something she couldn't, or maybe didn't want to, define.

Daniel was the type of man who drew attention wherever he went. Not just because he was six-four with broad shoulders but because of the way he carried himself, with purpose and confidence. He was also undeniably handsome. He had thick dark hair that always seemed to be in need of a trim, deep blue eyes that could be intensely focused or sparkle with humor, a sexy mouth that was quick to smile and a square jaw that, even when unshaven, was somehow appealing rather than scruffy.

Aside from all of that, he was a Garrett, and with the name came a certain amount of power and prestige. But instead of working at the furniture business owned by his family, Daniel had chosen to pursue a career in the field of computer science and was presently a network security specialist.

In high school, he'd been the boy that all the girls wanted to be with. Now that he was a man, he was even more coveted. But just a few hours earlier, he'd put a ring on her finger, and her gaze shifted now to the stunning princess-cut diamond solitaire. She knew it would take some time to get used to the weight of the ring on her finger; she wasn't sure she would ever become accustomed to its weight on her conscience.

"I just wish there was another way," she admitted.

"For me or for you?"

"Both."

"I told you I've got stocks and bonds worth at least two

hundred thousand. I could cash some of those in to pay for your sister's surgery."

And he would do it for her, too—no strings attached. Because that was the kind of guy he was. And as much as she hated taking anything from anyone—even a loan from her best friend—she would do it for Becca.

Her fourteen-year-old sister had been in her boyfriend's car when Todd lost control of the vehicle, which slid thirty feet down an embankment before crashing into a utility pole. The passenger side had taken the brunt of the impact, so while Todd had walked away from the scene, paramedics had to use the Jaws of Life to get Becca out of the mangled vehicle. She was rushed to hospital with three cracked ribs, a punctured lung and a tibial shaft fracture.

Three months later, it was discovered that the surgeon hadn't properly aligned the broken fragments of the fracture, and now Becca walked with a limp. After several more doctors' appointments and specialist consultations, it was agreed that another operation would be needed if she wanted to correct the problem. But because this surgery was considered elective, neither it nor the subsequent physiotherapy sessions would be covered by medical insurance.

A conservative estimate of the cost: eighty thousand dollars.

Just thinking about the enormity of the sum made Kenna's stomach cramp. While she'd finally paid off her secondhand car, she'd barely begun to make a dent in her student loans and the doctor wanted a fifty percent deposit before he would even book the surgery.

She hadn't had the first clue how she might scrounge up that kind of money, but she'd promised her sister she'd figure out a way. A lengthy conversation with their mother had garnered nothing but tears and regrets. Sue Ellen Duncan had always been good at both—it was handling her finances that proved to be a struggle. So when Daniel had stopped by to see Kenna later that night, she'd been desperate for a solution.

That was when he'd suggested they get married.

She'd stared at him blankly, waiting for the punch line, certain it had to be some kind of joke. He'd assured her that it was not. Kenna needed money for her sister's surgery; he wanted access to his trust fund; a quick ceremony in Vegas would give them each what they desired.

They'd been friends for so long that she sometimes forgot about the drastic differences in their backgrounds and social status. Which was ironic, considering that it had been such an impediment to their friendship in the beginning.

Aside from the fact that Daniel's family owned Garrett Furniture, his maternal grandfather, Jake Willson, had made a ton of money in real estate in the sixties. He'd spent as much of it as he could in his lifetime, left a substantial amount to his only child and put the rest into trust funds for his three grandsons.

Kenna's initial response to Daniel's proposal had been equal parts intrigue and revulsion. She liked the idea of earning the money, but the method he was suggesting made her wonder if she'd be selling herself, à la Julia Roberts in *Pretty Woman.* He immediately assured her that he was looking for a temporary marriage in name only—just one year out of her life in exchange for one hundred thousand dollars.

Or $273.97 per day to wear his ring on her finger.

She'd finally said yes.

Now as the taxi pulled up in front of the Courtland Resort & Casino, Kenna tried not to gawk. She'd never been to Las Vegas. In fact, she'd never ventured any farther from her hometown of Charisma, North Carolina, than Daytona Beach, Florida, so she experienced a little bit of culture shock just looking around.

The opulence of the luxury hotel was unlike anything she'd ever seen. Glossy marble floors, life-size statues, spectacular waterfalls and exotic flowers. It was like a tropical paradise inside a hotel lobby that was probably bigger than any other hotel she'd ever stayed in.

Check-in was expedited, no doubt by Daniel's platinum credit card, and although they each had only a small overnight bag, the desk clerk called for a bellman to assist with their luggage. The man, whose nameplate identified him as Alex, led them briskly down a wide corridor to a bank of elevators.

Each door of the elevator had an ornately scrolled *C* etched into the polished surface, and the doors opened without a sound. She stepped inside and noted there were specific buttons for Spa and Casino, but Alex pressed 7 and the elevator began its ascent. The ride was as smooth as it was quick, and then she was stepping out into a long hallway. The gold-and-cream decor continued here, from the patterned carpet beneath her feet and luxurious silk on the walls to the sconces that illuminated their path and the elaborately framed artwork along the way. The bellman slipped a key card into the slot of Room 722, and the lock released with a quiet click.

The first thing she noticed, with no small amount of relief, were the two queen-size beds that Alex informed her were custom luxury mattresses triple-sheeted with five-hundred-thread-count linens. The tablet on the bedside table controlled the lighting, the forty-inch flat-screen LCD TV, the iHome music system, programmable coffeemaker and draperies.

"Draperies?" Kenna echoed, not sure she'd heard him correctly.

In response to which he picked up the tablet and tapped the screen a few times, which caused the thick brocade curtains to slide across the floor-to-ceiling windows.

"Wow."

He smiled kindly. "Is this your first trip to Las Vegas, ma'am?"

"Yes," she admitted.

"Then we hope it's the first of many," he said. "And if there's anything at all we can do to make your stay more enjoyable, please don't hesitate to let us know."

"Thank you," she said.

Alex opened the drapes again, and she moved closer to the window, taking in the view of the Strip. Even this early in the day, the streets were bustling with activity. She couldn't wait to see it at night, lit up as it always was in the movies.

"The directory on the tablet has all the information you will require about the hotel—our three restaurants, spa services, shops and, of course, the casino."

He opened another door to reveal an Italian marble bath with deep soaker tub, separate glass-enclosed shower, double sinks, exclusive designer toiletries and thick Egyptian cotton towels on heated bars.

Daniel pressed a folded bill into his hand.

"Thank you very much, sir," Alex said, making his exit.

Kenna turned in a slow circle in the middle of the room, still trying to take it all in. "How long are we staying?"

Daniel chuckled at her obvious pleasure. "I only booked one night, but we can extend that, if you want."

"I want." She dropped onto the closest bed and let herself sink back into the mountain of pillows. Then she sighed. "Unfortunately, I have to work on Monday—and so do you."

He shrugged. "I could finagle a few extra days…if it was for a honeymoon."

She shook her head regretfully. "I can't."

He stretched out beside her, linked their fingers together. It was an easy, companionable gesture that nevertheless stirred something inside her. "You can't take a few extra days…or you can't marry me?"

"I can't take even one extra day." She squeezed his hand. "But I wouldn't be here if I wasn't planning to go through with the wedding."

She could almost see the tension leak out of his body. She knew his eagerness to tie the knot had nothing to do with love or happily-ever-after but was an indication of how much he wanted to accept Josh Slater's business proposition. For a five-million-dollar investment, he could be his friend's partner in the ownership of a professional stock car racing team under the banner of Garrett/Slater Racing.

"Are you sure?" he asked, giving her one last out.

She nodded. "Let's do it."

His brows lifted. "Do it?"

Belatedly she remembered that they were lying side by side on a queen-size bed, and she felt heat rise in her cheeks.

"Get married," she clarified, ignoring the awareness that hummed through her veins.

"Now?"

"Isn't that why we're here?"

"Sure," he agreed. "But we only got off the plane half an hour ago. I thought you might want to relax a little, maybe indulge in some of the hotel spa services."

"I don't think I'm going to be able to relax until this is done," she admitted.

"The wedding or the year?"

She managed a smile. "The wedding," she said, though she suspected the truth was both. The wedding was just a ceremony—a legal formality. Being married, presenting herself to their friends and families as Daniel Garrett's wife for the next twelve months, was going to be the true test.

"Did you want to at least go shopping first?"

"Shopping?" She looked at him blankly.

"The bellman mentioned there were shops downstairs, and since we're getting married, I thought you might want to wear something a little more weddinglike."

She glanced down at her white capris and sleeveless blue top with the ruffled placket, but shook her head.

His brows lifted. "No dreams of walking down the aisle in a white dress?"

She didn't let herself regret that she wasn't going to have the wedding she'd dreamed about since she was a little girl, because this wasn't a real wedding. "I don't want to pretend this marriage is something it's not."

"That's exactly what we're going to have to do," he reminded her gently.

"For everyone else," she acknowledged. "But not between us."

He shrugged. "Okay, then. Let's find a chapel."

He released her hand to pick up the tablet and found a link to a list of wedding venues—the number of which was astounding. And then there were countless ceremony options: traditional or themed, including disco, rock 'n' roll, country and western, pirates, vampires and even zombies.

"Kenna?" he prompted.

"I'd have to say it's a definite no with respect to pirates, vampires and zombies."

"How about walking down the aisle with Elvis?"

She shook her head. "Is there anything a little more... normal?"

He scrolled through a few more pages. "How about 'Traditional Elegance'?" He read from the description: "'This package offers a ceremony in our traditional chapel, with wedding music, bride's six-rose bouquet, groom's matching boutonniere, ten ceremony photos on CD, complimentary limousine service for the bride and groom to the marriage license bureau, and a witness, if required.'"

"That sounds good."

"Except that we were supposed to call at least forty-eight hours in advance to inquire about availability."

"Call," she suggested. "Maybe we'll get lucky."

He sent her a slow, heated look that had no doubt caused numerous women to tumble into his bed. Thankfully, a decade of watching him in action had immunized her to his charm and techniques. Mostly, anyway.

She smacked him in the arm. "Stop turning everything I say into a sexual innuendo."

"Stop saying things that sound like sex," he countered.

"You're a guy—everything sounds like sex to you."

"Probably true," he acknowledged unapologetically.

She looked at him now, her expression serious. "I know you want to get married, but are you sure you want to marry *me?*"

"I don't really want to get married," he reminded her. "But since that's what I have to do, I couldn't imagine marrying anyone else."

"A year is a long time to go without sex," she pointed out. "Especially for a man with a hedonistic reputation."

"My reputation is somewhat exaggerated."

"Somewhat?"

"Maybe the real issue isn't my reputation but that you don't think you can hold out that long. Because if you're suggesting an amendment to the terms of—"

"No," she said quickly, deliberately ignoring the leap of her pulse in response to his provocative statement.

He just grinned.

"I'm suggesting an amendment to the time frame," she clarified. "Six months should be long enough to convince people we tried to make our marriage work but realized we were better off as friends."

"Maybe most people," he acknowledged.

She knew he was excluding his parents from that list, and she knew he was right. After refusing his request for access to his trust fund only a couple of months earlier, David and Jane Garrett would definitely have suspicions about their son's sudden nuptials. And while she appreciated that Daniel didn't like deceiving his parents, she didn't understand how dragging the deception out over twelve months rather than six made it more palatable to him.

"Call about the chapel," she decided. "Let's make sure today is day one of my three hundred and sixty-five as Mrs. Daniel Garrett."

Daniel made the call.

Fifteen minutes later they were picked up by a limo that took them to the marriage license bureau, then returned them to the hotel for the ceremony.

When Kenna stepped inside the chapel, her breath actually caught in her throat.

Her groom halted beside her. "Is something wrong?"

"It's…beautiful."

"Why do you sound so surprised?"

"I guess I just thought… I mean, this is an impromptu wedding in Vegas. I expected Elvis in a polyester suit and—"

"You nixed the Elvis idea," he reminded her. "You wanted something more traditional."

She nodded, because it was true. But she hadn't expected something that would look and feel so much like a real church, with classic cathedral ceilings and antique stained glass, floral arrangements on marble columns and flickering candles everywhere.

The officiant started toward them. As he drew nearer, she noticed that he was wearing a clerical collar. Not an officiant, she realized, but a real minister, and his presence forced her to acknowledge the realness of the vows she was about to make.

He welcomed them, introduced himself as Gerald Laughton and inspected their marriage license. He'd just started to give them a brief rundown of the ceremony when a trim woman with neatly coiffed white hair and wearing an elegant rose-colored suit bustled in.

"Sorry, sorry, sorry," she breathlessly apologized. "I should have been here to greet you, but I got tied up waiting for a delivery from the florist."

"We weren't going to start without you," the minister assured her. Then to Daniel and Kenna he said, "This is Vera Laughton, the chapel administrator, your witness and my wife of thirty-four years."

After the introductions were completed, Vera took Kenna's arm and steered her away from the men, toward the back of the chapel.

"We've got a schedule to keep," she reminded them. "So let's get this started."

Vera handed Kenna a bouquet of flowers and signaled to a younger man with a camera around his neck. He punched a few buttons on the front panel of an intricate sound system and music began to fill the room.

Not Mendelssohn's "Wedding March" but Pachelbel's Canon in D Major, Kenna realized. She'd always thought it was a much more elegant and beautiful song, as she'd remarked to Daniel when they'd attended his cousin Braden's wedding several years earlier. Of course, Daniel wouldn't have remembered that. And even if he had, she would guess that the music had been chosen by the hotel's wedding coordinator or Vera—or maybe even the last bride who had walked down the aisle in this chapel.

But when Kenna drew in a deep breath and looked down at the hand-tied flowers in her hands, questions swirled in her mind. The website had indicated that the bride could choose between white or red roses, but she was holding a bouquet of soft pink gerberas—her favorite flowers.

In that moment, she knew that Daniel *had* done this. For her. He'd taken care of the little details to give her, if not the wedding of her dreams, at least one that she would remember fondly. And when she glanced up at the front of the chapel, where he was waiting more anxiously than patiently, she felt her heart swell.

When she'd first met him, back in high school, he'd been breathtakingly good-looking. At sixteen, he'd already been more than six feet tall and broad in the shoulders, but he'd added both muscle and maturity since then, and he was even more attractive now.

He rarely asked anything of her, and she knew he'd never wanted anything as much as he wanted Garrett/Slater Racing to become a reality. When she'd agreed to marry him, she'd thought she was doing it for Becca, but she realized now that she would have done it for him anyway. Because he wasn't just her best friend, he was a good man, and even if she wasn't *in* love with him, she did love him.

She started down the aisle toward him, and as her gaze met his, his lips curved. When she reached the front of the chapel, he took her hand and squeezed her icy fingers reassuringly. Or maybe he was holding on to her to make sure she didn't bolt.

She didn't look at him when he recited his vows, and she kept her gaze focused on his chin as she spoke her own. Because she wouldn't—couldn't—look him in the eye and say words that they both knew were a lie. Instead of "so long as we both shall live," the minister should have asked them to promise "until the monies of the trust fund have been released." It wouldn't have sounded nearly as romantic, but at least it would have been honest.

Thankfully, the ceremony was concluded fairly quickly. Then came the words that made both of them freeze.

"You may kiss your bride."

Her eyes lifted, and Kenna saw the knee-jerk panic she was feeling reflected in his. Obviously they'd both forgotten that after the exchange of promises and rings, there was supposed to be a ceremonial kiss.

He lifted one shoulder in a half shrug, then dipped his head and touched his mouth to hers.

The contact was so light and so quick, she might have

doubted it had even happened except for the fact that her lips actually tingled.

The slight furrow between his brows made her wonder if he'd experienced the same unexpected reaction to the fleeting kiss. Then he touched his mouth to hers again, lingering just a little bit longer this time, just long enough to start her heart racing.

When he drew back, she slowly exhaled the breath she'd been holding and forced a smile as the photographer circled around them, snapping photos.

"All part of the package," he reminded them.

Kenna's lips remained curved, presenting the image of a blissful bride as she posed with her now-rich husband.

But nerves danced and tangled in her belly, warning that she wasn't quite as immune to her groom as she wanted to be.

Chapter Two

Daniel had made reservations for dinner after the ceremony at Prime—a signature Courtland Hotel restaurant that specialized in steak and seafood. The decor was simple but elegant: leather armchair seating around square tables set with pristine white cloths, gleaming silver and crystal stemware all subtly illuminated by candlestick lamps.

Before they'd even opened their menus, the hostess returned to their table with a slim glass vase to keep Kenna's bouquet fresh. She was followed by the sommelier bearing a half bottle of champagne "compliments of the management" for the happy couple.

"To day one," Daniel toasted.

Kenna lifted her glass to tap against his. "Only three hundred and sixty-four more to go."

Maybe he should have been insulted that she was already so eager to end their marriage, except that he understood the circumstances of their union weren't what either of them would have chosen. All things considered, however, he knew he was a lucky man to have married the woman who wasn't just his best friend but one of the most beautiful women he'd ever known.

He looked at her now—at the pale blond hair that fell in gentle waves to her shoulders with a fringe of bangs above deep blue eyes. At the delicate shape of her face, the flawless complexion, and lips that were temptingly shaped and softer than he could have imagined. If he'd let himself imagine, which he definitely and absolutely had *not* until the minister had told him to kiss her. She was at least eight inches shorter than his six feet four inches, with a slender but undeniably feminine physique. And although she looked slight, he knew that she was strong and stubborn, genuine and loyal.

If he could choose to fall in love with anyone, he would choose Kenna. Instead, they'd chosen to follow the path of friendship, and falling in love now would force a detour from that path and ruin everything.

When the waiter came to their table, Daniel ordered the peppercorn steak with shrimp skewers, truffle mashed potatoes and steamed asparagus. Kenna selected the pan-fried sole with crispy fingerling potatoes and roasted cauliflower.

They chatted about inconsequential topics while they waited for their food, and while Kenna responded appropriately, she seemed more than a little distracted, and he couldn't help wondering if she already regretted her decision.

"If you're disappointed that Elvis didn't perform the ceremony, we can probably catch him on stage somewhere," he told her.

She smiled. "I'm not disappointed, and I thought the ceremony was lovely."

"Just not what you'd envisioned for your wedding day?" he guessed.

"Truthfully, I'd given up thinking that I'd ever get married."

"Why?" he asked, as the waiter approached with their meals.

"Too many frogs, not enough princes," she said, after the server had gone again.

"What about that guy you were dating from school? The gym teacher? You never did tell me why you broke up with him."

"While this marriage is a first for me, I'm pretty sure most husbands don't bring up the topic of their wives' ex-boyfriends on their wedding night."

"But we've already established that this isn't like most marriages," he said, unwilling to let her dodge the topic. "So what happened?"

She picked up her fork and poked at her fish. "Do you really want to talk about my failed relationships?"

He was pretty sure that was a rhetorical question, but he found that he did. He'd been so grateful when she'd agreed to marry him that he hadn't let himself question the fact that she was a beautiful, intelligent twenty-six-year-old woman who not only didn't have a steady boyfriend but very rarely went out on dates.

"I'm just realizing that you're probably as much of a commitment-phobe as I am," he told her.

"I don't know that any husband has ever spoken such romantic words to his wife."

The dryness of her tone made him smile as he cut into his steak. "I thought you were unhappy about being with me because you were thinking about him."

"Harrison and I broke up three months ago," she told him.

"But you thought he was the one." He popped a piece of sirloin into his mouth, chewed.

Kenna shook her head. "Not really. I *wanted* him to be the one, and then I realized that he wasn't."

"So you weren't thinking about him?"

"No," she said. "I was thinking—*hoping* that this marriage won't jeopardize a decade of friendship."

"It won't," he promised.

Yes, they were legally married, but that was just a piece of paper. And her new status as his wife aside, the woman sitting across from him was still the same woman he'd known for more than ten years, his best friend and most trusted confidante. There was no need for their altered marital status—or one little kiss—to change their relationship.

But they did have to do something about their living arrangements. "I'll ask Nate if I can borrow his truck when we get back."

She picked up her wine. "Why do you need his truck?"

"To move your stuff."

She set down the glass without drinking. "I'm not moving into your place."

He popped a shrimp into his mouth and wondered why she sounded genuinely startled by the idea. "My condo's bigger than your apartment," he said logically. "And I have two bedrooms."

"I know, but..." Her protest trailed off.

"But?" he prompted.

She just shook her head. "Obviously I didn't give the details of this arrangement enough thought," she admitted.

"What did you think—that we'd continue to live as we have been?"

"Of course not," she denied, but the color that filled her cheeks confirmed to him that was exactly what she'd thought.

"I agreed to separate bedrooms, not separate addresses," he said.

"But you don't have a bed in your second bedroom," she pointed out.

"We'll move my desk out and your bed in. If anyone asks why, we'll explain that we wanted to have a guest room for your sister when she comes to visit."

She considered this and finally, reluctantly, nodded. "But what if she really does want to come for a sleepover?"

"How often does she stay at your place?"

"Hardly ever," she admitted, stabbing a piece of cauli-flower with her fork.

"Then we'll worry about that if and when it happens."

She nodded, although not entirely happily, as she nib-bled on the tender-crisp vegetable. "Your condo is almost a half-hour drive from South Ridge High School," she pointed out. "I can be at work from my apartment in less than ten minutes."

"So you'll have to get up a little earlier in the morning," he acknowledged.

"I'm more concerned about how long my car will last with the extra miles I'll be putting on it every day."

"We'll get you a new one."

She frowned. "You're not buying me a new car."

"Why not?"

"Because."

He lifted a forkful of mashed potatoes. "What kind of an answer is that?"

"A valid one," she said stubbornly.

"Are you forgetting that I'm rich now?"

"I didn't marry you for your money."

"Actually, you did."

She flushed. "Okay, I did. But only for a small part of it and only for Becca."

"Because she needs the surgery," he acknowledged. "Just like she needed new shoes when you took that fifty bucks off me back in high school."

The color in her cheeks deepened. "She's a kid from a single-parent family in the wrong part of town—I just want her to have a chance."

"And she does," he told her. "Because she has you in her corner."

"And you," Kenna said. "You were the one who found Dr. Rakem."

"I just made some inquiries." He opened the folder the waiter had left on the table, added a tip and signed the tab.

"And then checked his references and arranged the consult."

He just shrugged, because it really hadn't been the big deal she was making it out to be.

"I don't know how to express how truly grateful I am," Kenna said softly.

"Getting naked might work," he said, because the mood had become entirely too serious and he wanted to see her smile.

Her lips did curve, even as she shook her head.

Then her gaze narrowed thoughtfully. "Actually, I've been thinking about our wedding night..."

His brows rose along with his interest.

"...and I decided it might be fun to strip—I mean, *see* the Strip."

And that quickly, his hopes were dashed.

"You want to play tourist, don't you?"

"Absolutely," she agreed.

He pushed his chair away from the table and offered his hand. "Then let's do it, Mrs. Garrett."

Seeing Las Vegas through Kenna's eyes was like seeing it for the first time all over again. She gaped at everything, from showgirls in glamorous costumes to working girls in almost nonexistent costumes; she paused to admire landmarks of famous hotels and the wares of unknown street artists; she sighed over a diamond bangle in the window display of Cartier but bought a rope-and-bead bracelet from a young boy's folding table.

She seemed as wary of the casinos as she was fascinated by them. When he fed a fifty-dollar bill into a slot machine and told her to pull the handle, she shook her head and tucked her hands behind her back, as if she was afraid to touch it.

He thought he understood her reticence. She'd grown up in a home where money had always been in short supply, so to feed it into a machine for the thrill of watching the drums roll and the lights flash and possibly—although not likely—hearing the bells clang was completely foreign to her.

"The key to gambling—whether it's slot machines or roulette wheels or card tables—is to never bet more than you can afford to lose."

"But a lot of people forget that, don't they?"

"Some get caught up in the excitement of the game," he acknowledged. "They forget that they're putting their money down for entertainment rather than an investment, and they get frustrated by their losses, certain their luck will change with the next hand, spin of the wheel or pull of the handle." He took her hand from behind her back, unfurled her fingers and wrapped them around the knob. "I promise I won't let you get carried away."

She looked at him and nodded, her fear of the machine outweighed by her trust in him. That unfailing trust was the double-edged sword that had kept him from acting on his feelings for her for the past decade, because he would never forgive himself if he hurt her. He pushed those thoughts—and his wants—aside and, keeping his hand over hers, pulled down the lever.

She held her breath as the reels spun, slowed and finally settled.

"I got a lemon, cherries and a bunch of grapes—what does that mean?"

"It means you lost."

"Oh."

"To win a single-coin bet on this machine, you need three matching symbols on the center line."

He prompted her to pull the lever again.

"Two oranges and a banana."

This time, she started the machine spinning on her own.

Cherries. Banana. Banana, cherries, grapes, orange, lemon.

The machine spit out five coins.

Her eyes lit up, and her obvious joy speared straight into his heart.

"What happened?"

"The fruit salad—" he pointed to the third icon "—is like a wild card that pays out every time."

"So I won."

"If you consider five coins winning," he said. "Actually, most slot machines don't even use coins anymore—they just keep track of credits and give you a receipt when you want to cash out."

"How much of your money am I losing every time I pull down this handle?" she asked him.

"Twenty-five cents."

"Oh." She smiled. "You can afford that."

He got a kick out of watching her watch the machine. The pulse in her throat would speed up as the drums spun around, her hands would clench into fists. He found himself mesmerized by that pulse point, tempted to touch his lips to it, to savor the warmth of her skin and taste her excitement. How would she respond if he did? Would her breath catch? Would her heart race? Would she realize she wanted him as much as he wanted her?

The drums stopped spinning and the excited light in her eyes dimmed just a little when the symbols didn't match.

She got a couple more payouts of five coins, but grew increasingly disheartened as his initial fifty dollar investment whittled down to forty, then thirty.

"You just keep pulling this handle until you run out of money?" she asked.

"Only if you want," he told her. "Some people believe certain machines are lucky, and if one they're playing doesn't pay out within a few spins, they move on."

"Maybe we should move on."

"Other people worry that, as soon as they walk away from a machine, it will pay out big on the first spin to the next player."

"Those are the ones who bet more than they can afford to lose," she guessed.

"Sometimes," he agreed.

She looked at the machine, considering.

"Three more spins," she decided.

The first spin earned her five more coins, the second nothing.

"Last one," she said, and pulled the handle.

Cherries. Cherries. Fruit salad.

The lights on top of the machine started to flash and bells and whistles sounded as the machine didn't just spit but spewed coins into the tray.

"Ohmygod. I won." She looked at him as if she wasn't quite sure she believed it, and her radiant smile wrapped around his heart.

"You did," he agreed.

Her eyes grew wide as the coins kept coming. "How much did I win?"

"$432.50."

"On a twenty-five-cent bet?"

"On a twenty-five-cent bet," he confirmed.

"Wow." That beautiful smile spread even wider. "Is this what they call beginner's luck?"

"Since the machine can't know you're a novice, I'd say it's more like lady luck."

"So the machine knows I'm a woman?"

He chuckled as he started to scoop the coins into a plastic bucket for her. "Touché."

When he was done, she stared at the coins that filled not just one bucket but three.

"Do you want to try another machine?" he asked.

She shook her head. "No, I just want to try the bed upstairs now." Then, realizing that he might interpret her words as an invitation—and although he knew better, he really wished they were—she hastened to clarify. "I mean I'm tired and want to call it a night."

"You're sure you don't want to give baccarat, poker or pai gow a go?"

"The only one of those I've even heard of is poker," she told him. "And yes, I'm sure."

He showed her where the cashier's window was so she could trade in her coins. When she walked away again, she had $451.75 in her hand—her winnings plus the remainder of what he'd put into the machine—and a jubilant smile on her face.

In the elevator on the way back up to their room, she peeled a fifty-dollar bill from her stack of money and handed it to him.

He didn't need the money, but he knew Kenna needed to not be indebted to him, so he took it from her and stuffed it into his pocket.

"I feel as if I've been on my feet all day," Kenna said, kicking off her shoes inside the door.

"Or at least the past ten hours." He couldn't help but notice that she had sexy toes, perfectly shaped and painted with shiny pink polish.

"I think I'm going to soak in that enormous tub for a while before I crawl into bed," she said.

He definitely didn't want to think about her in the tub—or be anywhere in the vicinity while she was. "In that case, I think I'll wander back down to the casino and see if I can lose some money at the blackjack tables."

"It's almost midnight," she pointed out.

"It's not even midnight and it's Vegas," he countered.

She shrugged. "Just as long as you don't lose my hundred grand."

"I won't lose your hundred grand," he promised.

But as he walked away, it occurred to him that they'd

already thrown the dice and risked something much more valuable than money—the status quo.

Kenna was rummaging through her overnight bag for her pj's when her cell phone chimed to indicate a text message. A quick glance at the screen revealed a brief note from Becca.

Can u take me to library 2morrow?

She could have texted back, but she decided to call her sister instead. She wanted to hear her voice, to remind herself of the primary reason that she'd become Mrs. Daniel Garrett.

After a brief exchange of pleasantries that warned Kenna her sister wasn't in a pleasant mood, Becca repeated her request.

"So can you take me tomorrow or not?" the teen demanded.

"Why do you need to go to the library?" Kenna asked.

"Research for a history paper."

"Don't you do your research on the internet?"

"Miss Roberts wants us to cite at least three hard-copy sources."

"What's your topic?"

"Revolution and Nationalism."

"That's a pretty broad subject."

"I'm supposed to pick one specific country as my focus," Becca admitted. "But I want to see how much material is available before I decide."

"When's the paper due?"

"Wednesday."

Kenna didn't even bother to sigh.

There was nothing she could say that she hadn't already said numerous times before, to no avail. Her sister was a smart kid who got decent grades without even trying, which

frustrated Kenna because she had no doubt that Becca would
be a straight-A student if she applied herself. Of course,
every time she tried to talk to her about college, her sister
brushed her off with a dismissive, "I'm not thinking about
college yet."

Kenna knew that if she didn't start thinking about it, and
seriously, it wouldn't ever happen. But that was a topic—
and a battle—for another day. All she said now was, "You
might want to ask Mom to take you to the library in the
morning so that you can get started on the paper, because
I won't be back until later in the afternoon."

"Where are you?"

"Out of town."

"That's an uncharacteristically vague answer," Becca
noted.

"I'll fill you in on the details later." When she'd figured
out how—and how much—to tell her sister.

"Oh." Her sister sounded intrigued. "Did you run away
for the weekend to have wild monkey sex with a stranger?"

She decided that outrageous question didn't even warrant
a response. "Can you ask Mom to take you to the library?"
she prompted instead.

"Not likely."

"Why not?"

"Sue Ellen's got a new boyfriend," Becca told her. "She
hasn't been home in three days."

Kenna forced herself to blow out a deep, calming breath.
"And you're only telling me this *now*?"

"It's no big deal."

"It *is* a big deal," she insisted. "You're only fourteen—"

"Almost fifteen," her sister interjected.

Which was still too young to be on her own for three
days. And three nights.

"You know you can always come and live with me." She
made the offer automatically, as she'd done several times
before. Only when the words were out of her mouth did

she realize that living with her now meant living with her and Daniel—and his condo didn't have enough bedrooms to make that work.

"I don't need a babysitter—just a ride to the library."

The dismissive response both relieved and frustrated Kenna. "I'll let you know when I'm on my way, but it probably won't be until about three o'clock."

"That's fine."

"You could get started on your internet research before then," she suggested.

"Sure," Becca agreed, without much enthusiasm.

Kenna said goodbye to her sister and disconnected the call.

She hadn't asked about the origin of Becca's bad mood. That the teen had asked her sister instead of her boyfriend for a ride to the library was enough of an indication that the on-again, off-again relationship with Todd Denney was currently off. And Kenna wasn't disappointed about that at all.

As she filled the oversize tub with bubbles, she acknowledged that she was hardly in a position to pass judgment on her sister's relationship. When she was Becca's age, she'd been completely and exclusively focused on her studies. That's not to say she never felt stirrings of attraction, but whenever she did, she forced herself to ignore them. She was terrified that if she gave in to those feelings she'd end up like her mother and her older sister, both of whom had got pregnant before they'd graduated high school.

Sure she'd harbored the occasional crush—even, briefly, on the man who was now her husband—but she'd never experienced the extreme highs and lows of teenage love and had no idea how to relate to her sister's angst. But not understanding didn't stop her from worrying. Todd was older and more experienced, and Becca was so infatuated that Kenna worried her sister would do anything to hold on to him.

As she lowered herself into the steamy water, she couldn't help but wonder if she wasn't guilty of the same thing—if her decision to marry Daniel wasn't just her way of holding on to him, at least for the next year. At the end of that time, they would end their marriage and go back to being just friends.

The concern for Kenna was what might happen between now and then—how living under the same roof and pretending to be a couple would change their relationship. Because it was inevitable that it would. They'd shared only one chaste kiss at the end of the ceremony, and already she was feeling things she didn't want to feel.

It wasn't the first time she'd experienced a tug of attraction in proximity to her best friend, but she was confident in her ability to ignore the unwelcome stirring of her body. It was the unexpected yearning of her heart that caused her more worry. When she was with Daniel, she felt the lure of something deeper, the longing for something more. But she'd never let herself even acknowledge those feelings because she knew they couldn't lead anywhere. Not even if he was now her husband.

As she stepped out of the bath and reached for a towel, she considered the possibility that she'd only imagined that tingle. That she might be romanticizing her relationship with Daniel because he was now her husband. Maybe the truth was that she hadn't felt anything at all but had manufactured a response because she wanted to feel something. Because she didn't want a fake marriage—she wanted a real wedding, a real husband and a real wedding night.

Tears stung her eyes as she rubbed the thick, fluffy towel over her body and wondered if she would ever enjoy the touch of a man's hands on her. But even more than the physical aspects of an intimate relationship, she longed to fall in love and be loved in return.

Since she was a little girl, she'd dreamed about the kind of family she'd never had. A man and a woman, married to one another, living together, sharing the joys and responsibilities of their children. She'd had other dreams, of course.

To go to college, which she'd done, and to become a teacher, which she'd also done.

But after half a dozen failed relationships, she'd finally accepted that the falling-in-love-and-having-a-family thing wasn't going to happen for her. So when Daniel suggested this marriage of convenience, she'd jumped at the opportunity, grateful at least for the illusion that she was in a normal relationship and could have a normal life.

But the fact that she was alone in a hotel room on her wedding night *proved* that it was nothing more than an illusion.

Chapter Three

Daniel's inaugural visit to Sin City had been with both of his brothers in celebration of his twenty-first birthday. Since then, he'd visited Las Vegas on several other occasions, usually with a group of buddies. He'd never brought a woman with him to Vegas, and he'd never imagined returning home with one as his wife.

But it was official now—he was married. And the band on his finger had been placed there by the woman who had been his best friend for the past ten years.

He shook his head. Even though it had been his idea, it was still hard to believe that Kenna was his wife.

He sat down at the blackjack table with a stack of chips, because he had nothing better to do. And how pathetic was that? It was his wedding night, his bride was in their room alone and he was playing cards.

Pathetic perhaps, but necessary. Because if he'd stayed upstairs with Kenna, he wasn't sure he'd be able to keep his hands off her. And he had no intention of crossing lines that had been firmly established more than ten years earlier just because one kiss had somehow stirred up wants and needs that he'd learned to ignore long ago.

As he pushed a chip toward the center of the table, the overhead lights glinted off the gold band on his third finger, making him pause.

"You'll sleep on the couch for a couple of weeks if you're gambling with the down payment for your house," the man sitting immediately to Daniel's left warned.

"What?"

"I saw you hesitate after you glanced at the ring," he explained.

Daniel knew a serious card player was always looking for clues about the other players at his table. Since he'd never taken the games too seriously, he didn't pay much attention.

"Name's Cal," the gray-haired man said, offering a hand. "But my friends call me Archie."

As he shook the man's proffered hand, he found himself thinking that the stranger looked somewhat familiar.

"Daniel Garrett," he said. "And we haven't even started to look for a house."

"Newlyweds," Archie surmised.

He nodded, unwilling to admit exactly how new. "Are you married?"

The old man shook his head. "No wife, just two exes."

Daniel signaled the dealer to "hit." He added a four of hearts to the jack of clubs and seven of diamonds, giving him twenty-one.

"Not a lot of players hit on seventeen," Archie noted. "I'm not sure whether that demonstrates confidence or recklessness."

"I'm not much of a gambler, but I figure playing it safe isn't really gambling, is it?"

"That's one perspective," the other man agreed. "And I guess if you don't care too much about winning, you can afford to lose."

Daniel only nodded and placed his next bet.

Archie played steadily, giving nothing of his thoughts or feelings away. He gestured his request for a hit or stay wordlessly, and alternately relinquished his bets or pulled in his winnings with equanimity.

Daniel slid another chip into betting position on the baize and wondered what Kenna would say if she knew the table he was sitting at had a hundred-dollar minimum. It was the same amount he'd won from his friends back in high school, after he'd bribed her with half to go out with him.

The dealer busted at twenty-two, paid out to the winners, then wished them all luck as she moved on to another table.

A new dealer came in and took up position, and Daniel considered calling it a night. He'd won more than he'd lost but, more important, he'd spent enough time at the table that his wife should be tucked into bed and sleeping by now.

A cocktail waitress sidled up to the table and set a glass of amber-colored liquid beside Archie. He nodded in acknowledgment and handed her a green chip.

"Thank you, Mr. Archer."

And Daniel suddenly realized why the man had looked familiar. "Calvin Archer—as in Archer Glass?"

"That's me," he confirmed.

Daniel decided to ante up. "You used to sponsor the number four-fourteen car."

"You're a racing fan," Archie noted, lifting his glass to his lips.

"I'm from North Carolina," Daniel said, as if that explained everything.

"Then you know about the scandal that forced Archer Glass to cut its ties with JB Racing."

Daniel nodded.

"I did what I had to do for the integrity of my company but, damn, I miss it." He shook his head.

"It gets into your blood, doesn't it?" Daniel said. "The sights, the sounds, even the smells. There's nothing like the excitement of race day at the track."

"You're right about that." Archie finished his scotch.

"So why hasn't anyone managed to draw you back into that excitement?" Daniel asked. "Because I know teams have tried."

"And how do you know that?" Archie countered.

"I've been doing some research, looking for a sponsor for Garrett/Slater Racing."

"Who?"

Daniel smiled. "Let me buy you a drink and answer that question."

Kenna didn't fall asleep easily.

Although the bed was undeniably comfortable, it wasn't her bed. And although she was alone, she knew that Daniel would be coming back to the room at some point. When he did, she thought she'd finally be able to sleep. But in the quiet darkness of the night, she was acutely aware of his every movement.

She heard the zip of his duffel bag being opened, then his muffled footsteps on the carpet, the click of the bathroom door and the pulsing of water in the shower. And that was when her naughty side took over, picturing him naked and wet, rubbing soap over his body, the lather sliding over his taut skin as the warm spray washed it away.

She'd seen him shirtless a number of times and had a pretty good idea of the basics. But since she'd never actually seen him naked, she gave her imagination free rein to fill in as required. And as her mind fleshed out those intriguing details, she finally drifted off....

The ring of his cell phone woke her up the next morning. Daniel snatched it up quickly, probably so that it wouldn't wake her, then he slipped out into the hall to have his conversation.

Kenna took advantage of his momentary absence to gather a change of clothes and take them into the bathroom. She dragged a brush through her hair, cleaned her teeth and quickly applied her basic makeup: eyeliner, mascara and lip gloss. Then she pulled on a pair of dark jeans and topped them with a pale pink T-shirt with lace overlay.

She was packing her toiletries into her bag when he came back into the room, pushing a room service cart.

"New job?"

He grinned. "I thought, if you were still asleep, you wouldn't appreciate a waiter strolling into the room."

"Good call."

He lifted the lids on the plates. "We've got eggs, toast, bacon, sausage, pancakes, fruit, yogurt, muffins, fresh juice and coffee."

"Oh." She feigned disappointment. "No French toast?"

His gaze narrowed. "Put the eggs on the toast," he suggested.

She smiled as she picked up a slice of bacon, bit into it. "So how much did you win?"

He poured two cups of coffee, pushed one across the table to her. "Sorry?"

"You were whistling when you came in last night, so I figured you must have won big."

He winced as he scooped eggs onto his plate. "Did I wake you?"

She shook her head. "I wasn't sleeping."

"Actually, I probably lost about three hundred. But—" his smile came back in full force "—I might have a line on a sponsor."

"Josh must be thrilled," she said, because she knew he would have shared the news with his soon-to-be partner right away.

"Cautiously optimistic." He added three sausage links and two pancakes to his plate. "We've had trouble finding a driver because we didn't have a sponsor, but no one wants to sponsor a team that doesn't have a committed driver."

She spooned berries on top of her yogurt, then threw

caution to the wind and snagged another slice of bacon. "So who is this sponsor?"

"*Potential* sponsor," he clarified.

She rolled her eyes as she sat down across from him. "Who is this *potential* sponsor?"

"Archer Glass."

"Randy Britton's old sponsor?"

"I'm impressed."

"Because I actually paid attention when you made me watch racing with you?"

He grinned. "Yeah."

"So when will you know if this *potential* sponsor is going to become an *actual* sponsor?"

"Hopefully soon." He got up to refill his coffee. "By the way, I had a message from Dr. Rakem this morning. He wants to do Becca's surgery on Thursday."

The abrupt shift in topic didn't surprise her half as much as the statement. "*This* Thursday?"

He nodded. "He had a cancellation so he offered to fit Becca in."

"But she hasn't even had her pre-op appointment—"

"Four o'clock tomorrow afternoon."

"I can't believe it." Even as her eyes filled with tears, she pushed away from the table and threw her arms around him. "Thank you."

"This is why we got married," he echoed her words.

She impulsively moved to kiss his cheek, except that he shifted his head at the same moment and her lips landed closer to the corner of his mouth than his cheek. Not on his mouth, but close enough that she felt that tingle again, from her lips all the way to the deepest part of herself.

She pulled back quickly, but his eyes held hers for a long moment, and she knew without a doubt that this time he'd felt the tingle, too.

But she didn't know what, if anything, either of them should do about it.

* * *

As Daniel and Kenna waited for their flight to board, he sensed her growing nervousness. He knew she was worried about sharing the news of their impromptu wedding with their families—probably his even more than her own.

Because of their long and enduring friendship, his brothers already thought of her as a sister and his parents treated her like a daughter, but the news of their elopement would undoubtedly raise eyebrows. She was worried that no one would believe that a decade of friendship had turned into something else, and he couldn't ignore her concerns. But he trusted that they could make this work, because they had that foundation of friendship, laid more than ten years before…

She wanted him to split the money and buy pizza out of his half?

He didn't know if he was insulted or impressed by her suggestion. But he wanted to spend time with her away from school even more than he wanted to win the bet, so he accepted her terms.

She suggested Mossimo's—a pizza place in her neighborhood—and he agreed because he knew she felt out of place with his usual crowd. He had no doubt that his friends would accept her, if only she would give them a chance, but he sensed it was going to take some time and patience to knock the chip off her shoulder.

They shared a medium pizza with pepperoni and hot peppers on his half, mushrooms and green peppers on hers, and a couple of sodas. When the pizza was delivered to their table, she slid a slice onto her plate, then picked off every single mushroom before she bit into it. He'd started on his fourth slice while she was carefully removing toppings from her second.

"Why did you order mushrooms if you don't like mushrooms?" he finally asked.

"Because I'm going to take the other two slices home for my sister, and she does like mushrooms."

"How old's your sister?"

"Four."

"And how old are you?"

"I'll be sixteen in December."

"That's quite an age gap," he noted.

She nodded. *"My mother says Becca is a lesson in what happens when you stop being careful."*

He had no idea what to say to that, so he backtracked. *"I guess if you're not even sixteen yet, you don't have your license."*

She shook her head.

"I'll be seventeen in January," he told her, though she hadn't asked.

"Did you get the car for your sixteenth birthday?"

"Yeah," he admitted. *"I wanted an SVT Cobra Coupe, but my dad said I would only get one of those when I could afford to buy it myself."*

She lifted her brows, and he knew without her having to say it that she expected—as a lot of people did—because his family was wealthy, he'd get whatever he wanted.

"My father has some pretty strong ideas about making sure his kids know—" he made quotation marks in the air with his fingers *"—the value of a dollar."*

"I bet even the car you're driving now cost more than a few dollars."

He nodded his agreement. *"And it gets me where I want to go, so I can't really complain."*

"I have to take three different buses to get to and from school," she admitted.

"That sucks."

"By the time I make all the necessary transfers, the trip adds almost an hour to the start and end of each day." She shrugged. *"On the other hand, it beats the alternative."*

"Walking?" he guessed.

To his surprise, she smiled as she shook her head. She really had a pretty smile. "Still being at South Ridge and feeling like I'm going nowhere."

When the waitress came to check on them, he asked for a box for her leftover pizza. She brought the box along with the bill, and he put some money on the table for payment, then counted out fifty dollars more and tucked them under the edge of the take-out box for Kenna.

Her eyes were riveted on the money, but she made no move to touch it.

"It's yours," he reminded her. "We had a deal."

She finally reached for the bills and tucked them into the front pocket of her backpack.

"I'm not usually so mercenary," she said, "but my sister needs new shoes."

He'd never known anyone like her. She was honest and genuine and completely unapologetic. Yeah, she had a bit of a chip on her shoulder, but from the little glimpses that she'd given him of her life over the past few weeks, he thought she'd probably earned it.

"So...do you think we could do this again sometime?" he asked.

She shook her head.

"Why not?"

"I'll admit that I no longer think you're a complete ass just because your family has boatloads of money, but the fact remains that we don't run in the same circles."

"Actually, if you want to get technical, it's yachtfuls of money."

Her lips tipped up, just a little, at the corners. "Which is too bad, because I almost think I could like you."

Then she pushed back her chair, and he immediately rose to his feet and offered her a hand. She seemed surprised by the gesture, but she put her hand in his, and he felt an unexpected warmth spread through him in response to the contact.

"I want to say 'hi' to someone in the kitchen before I head home," she told him.

"I can give you a ride."

She shook her head. *"Thanks, but I don't live far."*

"Are you sure?"

"I know where I live," she promised him, her blue eyes sparkling with humor.

He'd never known anyone else who had the ability to make him feel like an idiot with so little effort. But she wasn't ever mean about it and, truthfully, he kind of liked that she challenged him. Most of the girls he knew just nodded in agreement with everything he said. Kenna had her own thoughts and opinions, and she wasn't afraid to share them.

"I meant—are you sure you don't want a ride?" he clarified.

"I'm sure."

"Okay," he agreed, albeit reluctantly.

"Thanks again for the pizza," she said, and turned toward the back of the restaurant.

"Thanks for letting me win the bet."

It had been a long time after before he realized that he'd won a lot more than a hundred-dollar bet that day.

He only hoped he hadn't jeopardized everything by putting a ring on her finger.

When they landed at the Raleigh-Durham Airport Sunday afternoon, there was a text message on Kenna's phone from her sister.

@ library with Todd

Kenna sighed and simply replied ok.

It wasn't okay—not by a long shot, but she knew that expressing her disapproval of the relationship would only succeed in fueling her little sister's affection for him.

Besides, she had bigger things to worry about right now. Like Sunday night dinner at the home of her new in-laws.

David and Jane Garrett had bought a modest farmhouse set on ten acres of property when they were newlyweds. Over the years and as their family had grown, they'd renovated and added on so that the current dwelling bore little resemblance to the original structure. The first time Kenna had ever seen it, she'd loved it.

The two-story house was big but not particularly grandiose. Certainly no one seeing it from the street would think that it belonged to one of the wealthiest families in Charisma. But any time David complained that the floors were creaky and suggested they should move to a modern home in a newer neighborhood, Jane shot him down. "Each one of our boys took their first steps in this creaky old house, and I'm not selling those memories."

Kenna had a lot of happy memories of times spent in that house, too. Studying for numerous exams with Daniel at the butcher-block table; nibbling on warm chocolate chip cookies right out of the oven; playing flag football with his brothers and his cousins in the backyard; sitting on the porch swing with her head on Daniel's shoulder, trying not to cry the night before he left for college.

Because she'd spent so much time there over the years, no one was surprised when she showed up with Daniel Sunday afternoon. He'd wanted to get there early, so they could tell his parents about their marriage before everyone else arrived. Everyone else being his oldest brother, Andrew, Andrew's daughter, Maura, his girlfriend, Rachel, and middle brother Nathan.

But when they got to the farm, they discovered that Andrew and Rachel had beaten them there, eager to share the news of their engagement. Daniel sent Kenna a look, to which she responded with a subtle shake of her head, discreetly slipping her rings off her finger and into her pocket.

She knew they had to tell David and Jane about their

marriage, but she didn't want to steal the spotlight from Andrew and Rachel. Or maybe she was worried that having the light focused on Daniel and herself would reveal that they weren't head over heels in love as his brother and fiancée obviously were.

Nate showed up just as dinner was being put on the table, so the story of Andrew and Rachel's engagement was told again—in great detail by seven-year-old Maura—as platters and bowls of food were passed around.

No one made roast beef with all the trimmings like Daniel's mom, and it was usually one of Kenna's favorite meals. But today, as she listened to the discussion about potential dates and venues for Andrew and Rachel's wedding, she found herself moving more food around her plate than she put in her mouth.

Everyone was thrilled about the engagement. Of course, Andrew and Rachel had been dating since February—not a long time, really, but long enough to be sure that this was what they wanted. As Kenna watched their interactions, she couldn't help but see that there was a connection between them, so real it was almost tangible.

Beneath the table, Daniel gave her hand a questioning squeeze. She knew he was eager to share their news, because it was a prerequisite to accessing his trust fund, but the timing just seemed wrong to her. Or maybe, seeing the secretive looks and warm glances that passed between Andrew and Rachel, it was the marriage that seemed wrong.

Thankfully, with so many people around the table, there was rarely a lull in the conversation. There was discussion about Thomas Garrett's impending retirement and Nate's expected move to the CFO's office when he was gone; Andrew asked Kenna if she was looking forward to the end of the school year and her summer vacation, which prompted Maura to regale them with her plans to play soccer and take ballet classes and go to horseback riding camp; and then

Jane happened to mention that she needed to go shopping for a new dress for Lukas and Julie's wedding.

Lukas Garrett was one of Daniel's cousins who lived in Pinehurst, New York; Julie Marlowe was his fiancée, originally from Springfield, Massachusetts. Long before they'd decided to get married themselves, Daniel had asked Kenna to attend with him because he hated going to weddings on his own.

"When is the wedding?" David asked.

His wife rolled her eyes. "June twenty-first. Don't worry, I put the date in the calendar on your phone."

"That seems fast," Andrew noted. "They only met seven months ago."

Nate shook his head. "The Garrett men are dropping like flies. I think maybe I should lie low until this epidemic passes."

"Stop it," his mother admonished. "You should be so lucky to fall in love and share your life with someone one day."

"I'd say that Daniel and I are the lucky ones," Nate countered.

"Don't drag me into this," Daniel protested.

"Birds of a feather," his brother said. "With no intention of having our wings clipped."

"Do you feel as if your wings have been clipped?" Rachel asked Andrew.

"Only by choice," her fiancé assured her.

"And that's great for you," Nate said. "But it's not my choice."

"Never say never," Daniel cautioned.

"Whose side are you on here?"

"I'm not taking sides—I have nothing against marriage."

"Since when?" Nate demanded.

Under the table, Daniel gave her hand another squeeze. "Since Kenna and I got married."

Chapter Four

"Well, that was a disaster," Kenna commented, as they drove away from his parents' house toward her apartment.

"Actually, I thought it went pretty well," Daniel told her.

"Your mother *cried*."

"Not because we got married, but because we went to Las Vegas and didn't tell anyone."

She didn't look entirely convinced, but she let it go. "And now she wants to plan a big reception, so that we can celebrate with all of our family and friends."

"My mother does love to throw a party." And he kind of liked the idea of making a public statement about their marriage, letting the world know that Kenna was now his wife.

"You have to talk her out of it."

"Why?"

"Because I can't play the blushing bride in front of two hundred people," she told him. "Especially the single female contingent who will want to gouge my eyes out for taking you off the market."

"She won't invite two hundred people," he said, choosing to ignore the latter part of her statement.

Kenna just looked at him.

"Okay, she'll probably invite two hundred people," he acknowledged. "But so what? Did you really think we'd be able to keep the news of our wedding a secret?"

"No, I just didn't want anyone to make a big deal out of it." Those words were barely out of her mouth before her expression brightened. "Andrew and Rachel's wedding, on the other hand, should be a very big deal."

He'd always been impressed by the quickness of her mind and had to chuckle now. "Would you really throw my brother and his fiancée under the bus to save yourself?"

"It's not throwing them under the bus if they want to be there," Kenna pointed out. "Rachel wants the fancy wedding with all the trimmings—and Andrew wants to give her whatever she wants."

"He was in a bad place for a long time after Nina died," Daniel remembered. "It's good to see him so happy again."

She nodded, because she'd been there through that difficult period after his eldest brother had lost his wife, and she'd shared his worry.

"Don't you want that for yourself?" she asked him now. "To get married because you're in love?"

"I'm already married," he reminded her.

"And what if you meet someone now?"

"Huh?"

"What if you walk into a coffee shop tomorrow and bump into the woman you were meant to spend the rest of your life with?"

"If it hasn't happened in the past twenty-seven years, I don't think it's going to happen tomorrow or any other time in the next twelve months."

"But it could," she insisted.

"If we were really meant to be together, I'd just explain

to her that we have to wait until my divorce is final to fall madly in love."

"You're making fun of me."

"Yes, I am," he agreed. Because the scenario she was proposing was ridiculous—because there really was no one he could imagine wanting to be with more than he wanted to be with Kenna.

"It could happen," she insisted.

"It's just as likely that you might meet someone," he told her.

"Yeah, because guys are always lining up to go out with high school science teachers. I practically trip over them trying to get to my classroom."

"I believe it," he told her. "Not because you're a high school science teacher, but because you're smart, fun, kind, loyal, generous and beautiful."

"If I ever decide to join luvmatch-dot-com, you're writing my profile."

"But mostly—" he looked at her and grinned "—because you look really good in a skirt."

After dinner, Daniel had not only convinced Nathan to let him borrow his truck, he'd somehow cajoled his brother into helping him move some of the bigger items that Kenna wanted from her apartment. So while they were taking apart her bed, she boxed up her clothes and personal items and took them over to his condo.

She'd just started unpacking when there was a knock on the door. Although she hadn't expected they would be so close behind her, Kenna didn't consider that it might be anyone other than her new husband and his brother—until she opened the door and discovered her mother-in-law standing on the other side.

"Mrs. Garrett, hi."

"Can I come in?"

She stepped away from the door. "Of course."

"This is for you," Jane said, offering a vase overflowing with colorful blooms.

"It's gorgeous," Kenna said. "Rachel's work?"

Daniel's mother nodded. "One of the benefits of having a florist as a future daughter-in-law is that I didn't have to wait until business hours tomorrow to offer an apology."

Kenna took the arrangement into the dining room and set it in the middle of the table. "But why are you apologizing?"

"Because I know I seemed less than thrilled about the announcement of your marriage."

"There's no need to apologize—I know the news was a surprise."

"But not an unpleasant one," Jane assured her. "I always suspected that Daniel never fell in love with any of the girls he dated because of his feelings for you—not that he was ever willing to acknowledge those feelings, but I could see that they were there."

Her claim confirmed Daniel's suspicion that his mother wanted to believe their marriage was real. But Kenna didn't know whether that was because she'd been married for forty years and believed in happy endings, or because it was preferable to suspecting that her youngest son had ulterior motives for his marriage.

"So you can understand why I was beginning to wonder if he'd ever meet that special someone...and why I'm so glad that someone was you."

Jane took both of Kenna's hands and held them, her gaze steady and sincere.

"I know I should welcome you to the family, but you've been part of our family for ten years already. So instead I'm going to tell you both David and I are overjoyed that your membership in our family is now official."

Kenna's throat tightened as Jane released her hands and drew her into her embrace.

Daniel's parents had never been anything but warm and welcoming, and she'd loved them from the start. And Jane's words would have meant so much to her if she and Daniel had married for all the right reasons; if the vows they'd exchanged had been more than a means to an end. Instead, his mother's genuine warmth and acceptance made her want to cry.

"And if you have no objection," Jane continued as she released her, "I really would like to host a reception to celebrate your wedding."

Kenna had a whole boatload of objections, but none that she could admit to Daniel's mother without raising red flags.

"Of course, your mother might already be planning something," Jane realized. "But I'd be happy to coordinate with her."

"Actually, we haven't told my mother yet," Kenna said. "But I don't think that's a concern, anyway."

"Good, because I don't want to step on any toes, but I know there are so many friends and family who would appreciate the opportunity to give you their best wishes."

"My only suggestion would be to wait until after Andrew and Rachel's wedding."

"But they just got engaged—they haven't even set a date yet," Jane protested.

"Andrew doesn't want to wait too long," Kenna reminded her of the discussion that had gone on at the dinner table. "But Rachel wants a big wedding with all the bells and whistles, and that's going to take a lot of planning."

Apparently Daniel was right—when it came to self-preservation, she would absolutely throw his brother and future sister-in-law under the bus.

Jane sighed. "You're right. And with Rachel's parents living out of state, she might appreciate some help."

"She'll be thrilled," Kenna said, confident that it was true.

"Then we'll plan a reception for you and Daniel next summer—to celebrate your first anniversary," Jane decided, apparently willing to postpone but not relinquish that plan.

"Sounds good," Kenna said, and sent up a silent prayer that her temporary mother-in-law would someday forgive her for the lie.

Because by next summer, Kenna and Daniel's marriage would be over.

As Daniel stepped out of the shower Monday morning, he was confident in his ability to adjust to life as a married man. Granted it was only day three, but so far their legal status as husband and wife hadn't changed much of anything between Kenna and him. They each had their own lives, and he expected that they would continue to live those lives. True, they were now living under the same roof, but so long as he remembered this was a marriage in name only and ignored the hum of attraction, the proximity shouldn't cause any real problems.

He wrapped a towel around his waist and stepped out of the bathroom, breathing in the heady scent of freshly brewed coffee. Okay, that was a change, but having someone else start the coffee in the morning was an adjustment he didn't mind making. And if she wanted to cook breakfast, he wouldn't object to that, either.

Maybe it was because his mind was preoccupied with thoughts of bacon and eggs, or maybe it was because he hadn't yet had his morning hit of caffeine, but whatever the reason, he forgot that living with his wife had required making space for her things until he reached into the top drawer of his dresser for a pair of boxers and found his hand enveloped in soft, frothy lace.

His eyes opened wide to stare at the tiny scrap of pale shimmery blue fabric—and he felt a subtle but distinctive stirring of interest low in his belly.

The rational part of his brain wanted him to drop the garment back into the drawer and pretend he'd never seen it. The depraved part was suddenly trying to paint a picture of Kenna wearing nothing more than the panties in his hand—a mental image that was both incredibly arousing and distinctly unnerving.

Kenna's status as his wife was temporary and in name only. Much more important was the fact that she was his friend, which meant that he definitely should *not* be thinking about her in her underwear.

They weren't sharing a bed—they weren't even sharing a bedroom. But in order to maintain the illusion that theirs was a normal marriage, they'd decided that Kenna's clothes would hang beside his in the closet and he'd empty out a couple of drawers in his bureau for her use. For a brief moment this morning, he'd forgotten that.

He pulled the drawer open farther to return the undergarment to its proper place, and discovered a riot of color and texture. There were pastels and brights, smooth satins and delicate laces, polka dots and animal prints, many of them decorated with little bows or sparkly beads.

He'd never given much thought to what Kenna wore beneath her clothes. Her status as his best friend forced him to steer away from thoughts in that direction. He couldn't deny there'd been some curiosity—because yeah, he was a guy and it was unnatural *not* to wonder—but he'd never let his mind wander too far down that forbidden path. His mind was definitely wandering now…and that subtle stirring wasn't so subtle anymore.

He had a close and intimate acquaintance with women's lingerie. He could unfasten a front clasp as easily as he could back hooks; he knew the difference between a G-string and a thong; he appreciated that push-up bras enhanced a woman's attributes and despised padded bras for false advertising.

He found himself examining a bra of purple satin overlaid with black lace, thinking that the deep color would provide a stark contrast to her pale skin, and the scallop-edged cups would entice a man to discover what was inside. He definitely wouldn't mind seeing what she looked like in it… and then out of it.

"There's French toast in the…" Kenna's words trailed off when she spotted the bra in his hand. "What are you doing?"

"Trying not to think about how you'd look in this," he admitted.

Color stained her cheeks as she snatched the bra out of his hand, stuffed it back in the drawer and pushed it firmly shut. "Stay out of my underwear."

He grinned. "I never gave much thought to getting into them…until about three minutes ago."

"Well, stop thinking about it," she advised. "Just because I'm your wife doesn't mean I'm going to get naked with you."

"A crazy idea," he agreed.

Her lips twitched in response to his dry tone. "Almost as crazy as the two of us getting married."

"But we did that anyway," he pointed out.

"You set out the terms," she reminded him. "A one-year marriage on paper only."

He had set out the terms—desperately and impulsively. And he would have offered her anything, agreed to anything, because getting her to that chapel in Vegas had been a prerequisite to the release of his trust fund. But agreeing to twelve months of marriage on paper only when he'd already been celibate for more than six had not been a well-thought-out plan.

Especially now that he'd seen his wife's underwear.

"What if I want to renegotiate?" he asked.

Kenna shook her head. "Not going to happen."

He took a step closer, deliberately invading her personal space. "You know me well enough to know that I can't resist a challenge."

She held up a hand, no doubt to push him away, but her palm hovered in the air, as if reluctant to touch his bare skin. Her gaze dropped to the towel slung around his waist, and her breath hitched.

Clearly his wife wasn't as unaffected as she wanted him

to believe. He caught her wrist and pressed her palm against his chest, so she could feel his heart pounding against his ribs.

She moistened her lips with the tip of her tongue, drawing his attention to the tempting curve of her mouth. And he *was* tempted. Since the brief kiss they'd shared in that Las Vegas chapel, he'd spent an inordinate amount of time thinking about the lushness of her mouth, wanting to sink into the softness, savor her sweet flavor.

One simple kiss had blown the boundaries of his relationship with Kenna to smithereens, and he didn't know how to reestablish them. Or even if he wanted to.

"Aren't you the least bit curious about how it might be between us?"

"No," she said, though her inability to meet his gaze made him suspect it was a lie. "I'd prefer to maintain my unique status as one of only a handful of women in Charisma who haven't slept with you."

"I haven't slept with half as many women as you think," he told her.

She lifted her brows. "Half of a thousand is still…ick."

His eyes narrowed. "You know I've never been that indiscriminate—and I know what you're doing."

"What do you think I'm doing?"

"Deflecting the conversation. Pretending you don't feel the pull between us. Trying to annoy me so that I stop wondering what you're wearing under that dress."

"And maybe you're flirting with me to keep me from worrying about my sister's doctor's appointment this afternoon."

"I'm not that noble," he assured her.

She shook her head, but the hint of a smile tugged at the corners of her mouth. "There's French toast and bacon in the oven, if you want it."

"I want to know if you really wear that stuff."

"No, I just buy it to take up storage space and torture your imagination."

"You're a cruel woman, Mrs. Garrett."

She tossed a saucy smile over her shoulder. "Have a good day, Mr. Garrett."

When Kenna was gone, he poured himself a mug of coffee and sat down with the hot breakfast she'd left for him.

It was day three—only three hundred and sixty-two more to go.

He had a feeling the next year was going to be the longest year of his life.

Kenna was considering how to tell her colleagues about her weekend wedding as she waited for the staff-room coffeepot to finish brewing. She was pouring the first cup when Laurel Bane, her close friend and a fellow teacher, came into the staff room.

"Oh. My. God."

The excitement in her friend's voice nearly made Kenna spill her coffee. "What?"

Laurel grabbed her hand, her attention obviously snagged by the diamonds flashing on Kenna's finger. "When did this happen?"

"Saturday," she told her friend. "In Las Vegas."

"Wow." Laurel enveloped her in a fierce hug. "And congratulations."

"Thanks."

Then Laurel smacked her in the shoulder with the back of her hand. "I can't believe you got married without telling me."

"We didn't tell anyone," Kenna said.

Her friend sniffed. "Nobody?"

"Nobody," she confirmed.

"Okay, then," Laurel relented, lifting the pot to pour coffee into her own mug. "I'll forgive you *if*...you give me all the juicy details of your wedding night."

Kenna felt her cheeks flush. "I guess you're going to have to learn to hold on to a grudge, then."

She added two spoonfuls of sugar to her coffee, stirred. "Okay, just give me a couple of really good adjectives to describe Daniel's manly parts."

It was only then that Kenna realized she'd never told her friend who she had married. "How did you know I married Daniel?"

"Please," Laurel said. "As if the size of the rock wasn't a big enough clue, I always knew there was more between you two than friendship."

This echo of Jane Garrett's claim made Kenna wonder if other people imagined that they saw the same thing. If it was so unusual for men and women to be friends that there was always the assumption of deeper feelings beneath the surface. But she wasn't going to let anyone else's assumptions influence her reality—her friendship with Daniel was too important to her.

"So how was *your* weekend?" she asked, eager to change the topic of conversation.

"Not nearly as eventful as yours."

"Didn't you have a date with…" She trailed off, trying to remember the name her friend had mentioned.

"Roger," Laurel supplied.

"And?" Kenna prompted.

"And the experience reminded me that I hate dating."

"So why do you do it?"

"Because I'm still foolishly optimistic enough to think that someone will sweep me off my feet someday."

"Then maybe you should go out with the janitor," Kenna couldn't resist teasing.

"Go ahead—laugh at my humble desires and then go home to your hunky husband."

"I wasn't laughing," she denied. "Okay—I was, but only at the mental image, not your desire to fall in love."

Because she understood exactly how her friend was feeling. Not that she could admit it, of course. Laurel might be one of her best friends, but Kenna still couldn't tell her the truth about her marriage.

"Why aren't there more guys like Daniel out there?" Laurel wondered aloud. And then her expression brightened. "You know, it just occurred to me that a sweet and sexy guy like Daniel must have some equally sweet and sexy friends."

"Weren't you, just last week, talking about how much you hate being set up? How the next time someone tells you that she knows a guy 'you just have to meet' you're going to run in the opposite direction?"

Her friend waved a hand dismissively. "Those rules don't apply to you because you've proved you're a true friend by not pushing me toward any pathetic-slash-desperate-slash-creepy guys."

"You do know you don't have to go out with any of those guys if you don't want to?"

"I know," Laurel admitted. "But I'm afraid that if I turn any one of them down, he might be 'the one,' and I really want to get married."

"Why the sudden urgency to find a husband?" Kenna asked.

Laurel sighed. "Because it's my birthday at the end of the month."

"I know—you circled the date on my calendar and told me that we're going out for drinks."

"But I didn't tell you that it's my *twenty-ninth* birthday."

"So?"

"So next year I'll be thirty, and it's a well-documented fact that a woman who isn't married by the time she's thirty probably won't ever marry."

"Documented by whom?"

Her friend shrugged. "I don't remember."

"Laurel, you've got to stop believing everything you read on the internet," she chided gently.

"I don't want to be living alone with a dozen cats when I'm eighty."

"Nobody does," Kenna agreed.

And she wasn't entirely without sympathy because she knew it was possible she could end up in the same situation. But if she did, at least now she'd be able to say that she'd once been married.

Chapter Five

Daniel had given a business card with all of his contact information to Cal Archer and was hoping to hear from him about the proposition they'd discussed in Las Vegas. But when Archie called Monday afternoon, he didn't want to talk about Garrett/Slater Racing but the title on Daniel's card.

After a brief greeting, he said, "So what's a network security specialist?"

"Basically a computer administrator who specializes in protecting a company's data and other information."

"Do you build firewalls?"

"That's one aspect of what I do," Daniel told him.

"I've been told I need a new firewall. I don't even know what that means."

"A firewall protects against hackers and malicious software. It's like a barrier between your computer and the internet. But even with a firewall, you need someone to monitor your network for breaches in security."

"My son, Joe, takes care of that. He found the breach."

"Did you want me to talk to him?" Daniel asked, still trying to determine the purpose of the call.

"No, I want you to come and look at my system, assess the security and tell me what I need to do to fix it."

"Isn't there someone local you usually work with?"

"Yeah, but he's obviously not doing his job if someone got in, is he?"

"I'm not sure that's obvious," Daniel told him. "It depends on the level of security that was in place and how it was bypassed. No system is one hundred percent foolproof, which is why security measures need to be updated regularly."

"We've got a major proposal that we're working on—a bid to supply the doors and windows for a new condominium community. Joe suspects that the hacker works for a rival company that wants a peek at our paperwork in order to underbid us."

Daniel didn't dismiss Cal's concerns. He knew of companies that had been hacked for less.

"I'm not asking as a favor. I'm willing to pay the usual rate for your time, including travel, and your expenses. And—" Archie dangled the carrot "—maybe we'll have a chance to discuss your other business proposition in more detail when you're here."

"I'll book a flight and get back to you."

Life was good, Daniel thought, as he sat down to a plate of garlic lemon shrimp with pasta Monday night.

Gone were the days of coming home from work to put a frozen dinner in the microwave. Although he hadn't proposed to Kenna because she knew her way around a kitchen, he appreciated that she did.

Of course, their first disagreement as a married couple had been with respect to the division of labor when he'd suggested that Kenna, being the much better cook, should be in charge of making dinner every night and he could take care of the cleanup. She'd argued that the first person home at the end of the day should be responsible for starting the meal, although she did agree that the cook should be excused from cleanup. Since her schedule was much more defined than his and meant that she'd usually be home first, he agreed.

And now he was reaping the benefits of a delicious meal prepared by his wife. Only a few months earlier, he'd balked at the idea of marrying in order to gain access to his trust fund. He'd told his brothers that he had no intention of tying himself down to one woman for any reason—and he'd meant it.

But when the generic concept of a wife began to take the specific form of Kenna in his mind, he found that he wasn't so opposed after all. As she sat down across from him at the table now, he wondered if his marriage was evidence that he'd changed his mind…or had a change of heart.

"How did it go with Dr. Rakem today?" he asked.

"Good, once we finally got there."

"Did you have trouble finding his office?"

"No, the only trouble was trying to tear Becca away from Todd." She speared a shrimp with her fork. "They came out of the school attached at the hip like they were in a three-legged race. I don't think I'm a prude, but the way she lets him touch her in public makes me shudder to think what they do in private. But maybe I shouldn't be surprised, considering she lives with the example of a mother who throws herself at any good-looking guy who walks by."

"And the appointment?" he prompted, because he knew Kenna well enough to know that letting her continue on that tangent would only get her riled up.

"Dr. Rakem is confident the surgery will be a success. Becca is excited and afraid, I think. Not about the operation so much as the possibility it won't fix the problem. And I can tell she doesn't want to get her hopes up."

"Because hope can result in disappointment," he guessed.

She nodded. "And she's already had so much disappointment in her life."

And because he knew a lot of that could be traced back to her mother, it seemed logical to ask, "Did Sue Ellen have any concerns about the procedure?"

"Only about who was paying for it."

He could tell by her tone that she was more disappointed than surprised by her mother's attitude.

"How did she respond to the news that we got married?"

"She was overjoyed that her daughter finally snagged 'that handsome Garrett boy.'"

"And by 'handsome' she meant 'rich'?" he guessed.

Kenna managed a smile. "Although you are undeniably handsome, too. And thankfully she has no clue how rich you really are—or soon will be."

"What was Becca's reaction?"

"She's always liked you, so she was cool with it." She pushed her pasta around on her plate. "Other people are a lot less so."

"What other people?"

"People who read about our nuptials on Facebook."

"You put a relationship status update on your Facebook page?"

She shook her head. "Laurel posted a 'congratulations' message on hers in the morning, and by lunchtime I'd received fifty-three messages—most of them from women who wanted you for themselves."

"Only fifty-three?"

"There were well over a hundred by the end of the day."

"The joys of social networking."

She nibbled on a bite of pasta. "So how was your day?"

"Interesting," he said. "I got a call from Cal Archer today."

"About the sponsorship?"

He immediately shook his head. "It has nothing to do

with GSR. He wants me to go to Kentucky to perform a security assessment of his business network."

It wasn't uncommon for him to travel for work. S3CUR3 N3TW0RKS had several big clients in North Carolina, but most of them were within a hundred miles of Charisma. So while he was often out of town during the day, it was rare for him to go out of state, even rarer just for a consult.

Of course, he wasn't accustomed to having to clear his plans with anyone and it hadn't occurred to him, until just now, that maybe he should have conferred with her before he'd booked his flight.

Because Kenna knew what his job entailed, she immediately recognized that this was an unusual situation. "Don't they have people who can do that in Kentucky?"

"You would think," he agreed. "But Archie did suggest that we might discuss the sponsorship, as well."

"Then it's definitely worth the trip."

"So you're okay with this?"

"Why wouldn't I be?"

"Because we just got married."

"Before I moved in here—yesterday—I'd been living on my own for three years," she reminded him. "I think I can manage a few days without you."

"It won't be that long. No later than Thursday, for sure." He got up from the table and carried his plate to the sink. "But my flight leaves early, so I should pack."

She pushed back her chair, blocking his path. "*After* you do dishes."

"But—"

"Your deal," she reminded him.

And because it was, he did the cleanup.

Kenna requested a substitute to cover her last two classes on Thursday so she could see Becca before her sister went in for surgery. Sue Ellen was there, too, tears streaming down her face as she waited for her youngest daughter to be taken to the O.R. Thankfully Becca was so accustomed to her mother's drama that the wrenching sobs didn't faze her.

Determined to be strong for her sister, Kenna kept her chin up and her gaze steady. "I'll be here when you wake up," she promised.

"Okay."

Kenna stepped back, but as the attendants started to wheel her bed out of the room, Becca reached for her hand.

"Thank you."

"I love you, Becca."

Her sister's smile wobbled at the corners. "Back atcha."

She settled into the waiting room with a stack of test papers that needed to be marked before the end of term. Though she didn't expect she'd be able to concentrate enough to get much work done, she needed something to help pass the time.

Sue Ellen had nothing to occupy her hands or her mind, so she paced. And she didn't pace quietly. Her high heels clicked on the linoleum floor, the bracelets on her wrist jangled and she let out frequent and heavy sighs.

Kenna endured twenty minutes of this before she finally said, "Why don't you sit down? You're going to wear out the floor before Becca's out of surgery."

"Sit?" Sue Ellen protested. "How can I sit while some doctor's cutting into my baby girl?"

"You focus on the fact that the doctor is a specialist and accept that stomping around isn't helping anyone."

Her mother's pretty blue eyes filled with shimmery tears. "It's easy for you, isn't it?" She sniffed. "You don't have to worry about anything anymore."

"I'm as worried about Becca as you are," Kenna told her.

"But you don't have to worry about how you're going to pay the bills because you had to give up a shift at work to be here." Sue Ellen sniffed again. "Belinda was happy enough to take my hours at the diner, but she wouldn't give me any of hers."

Kenna had no idea who Belinda was, and she didn't care. "How many shifts did you give up when you were with Charles last weekend?"

"That isn't any of your business."

"You're right—except when you abandon your 'baby girl' for three days."

"I did no such thing," her mother denied indignantly. "And where were you last weekend? Oh, that's right— getting married. Not that you bothered to tell your mother about your plans."

She sighed. "Can we not do this right now?"

A single tear tracked slowly down Sue Ellen's cheek. "I never had a wedding of my own—and you didn't even let me be part of yours."

Kenna was tempted to point out that her mother had never had a wedding because she preferred to sleep with other women's husbands rather than finding her own, but she bit down firmly on her tongue. While Sue Ellen was obviously in a mood to rant and rave, Kenna preferred to focus on her sister.

"You're not even sorry, are you?" Sue Ellen demanded.

"What am I supposed to be sorry about?"

"Not inviting me to your wedding."

"No one was invited," she told her mother. "Daniel and I wanted a quiet, private ceremony."

Sue Ellen wasn't mollified by the explanation. "Don't think people won't be counting on their fingers anyway."

"What?"

"The number of months that pass until the baby is born."

"I'm not pregnant," Kenna said.

"Of course that's what I've been telling people, too," her mother said in a conspiratorial tone.

"No, Mom. I'm really *not* pregnant."

"Then why…" She let the question trail off, a genuine look of puzzlement in her eyes.

"Why did Daniel marry me?" Kenna suggested.

"Well…yes."

She was tempted to tell her mother that there were 6.5 million reasons, not one of which was a baby. Instead, she went with the response they'd manufactured to answer that exact question. "We got married because neither of us could imagine a life without the other one in it."

"You really do love him?"

She nodded, because while she wasn't *in* love with him, she really did love him.

Of course her mother, ever the pragmatist, said, "Then you shouldn't waste any time getting pregnant. That way if he leaves you, at least you'll get child support."

He'd intended to be at the hospital before they took Becca down for her surgery, but a delayed flight into Kentucky meant even more of a delay for Daniel's outward-bound flight on the same plane. He went straight to Mercy Hospital from the airport, making only a brief stop at the café on the main floor before tracking Kenna down in the surgical waiting room.

She was sitting at one end of a vinyl sofa with a stack of papers in her lap. Her head was down, her hair curtaining her face, but he could see the tension in every line of her body. She must have heard his footsteps, because she glanced up and saw him in the doorway.

She gave him a weary smile. "Hey—when did you get back?"

"My plane landed about an hour ago." He offered her one of the cups he carried—a tall cinnamon dolce latte. "How are you holding up?"

"I'm fine," she told him.

"Becca will be, too," he promised, lowering himself into the empty seat beside her. "Dr. Rakem's one of the best."

She nodded. "I know. But she's only fourteen…and she was so brave, but I know she's scared."

She wouldn't appreciate false assurances or empty promises, so he only slid an arm across her shoulders. Kenna let her head fall back, against his chest.

"Thanks for being here," she said.

"I'm sorry I wasn't here earlier." He sipped his coffee. "Have you been waiting by yourself the whole time?"

She shook her head. "Sue Ellen was here for a while. She had to sign all the consents and waivers, but then she said it was too stressful for her, the sitting around and waiting."

Her tone was neutral, but he'd known her long enough to recognize the anger and frustration she kept carefully hidden.

The first time she'd ever mentioned Sue Ellen, he hadn't realized she was talking about her mother. But the more time he spent with her, the more he realized that theirs was hardly a typical mother–daughter relationship.

He didn't doubt that Sue Ellen loved her daughters, but she definitely had her priorities screwed up. Even back in high school, it was often Kenna who had to remind her mother to pay the bills so their power wouldn't be cut off or to pick up groceries so she could pack lunches for both herself and Becca.

"Do you ever think about one seemingly inconsequential event in your life and wonder 'what if' something had happened differently?" she asked him now.

"Anything in particular you're wondering about?"

"Mr. Taylor's chemistry class," she admitted. "I don't know if it was luck or fate that he assigned us to be lab partners, but I will always be grateful to him for that."

"Me, too," he said. "I wouldn't have done nearly as well in that class without you."

Her lips curved. "You did suck at chemistry."

"Or maybe I pretended to suck at it so you'd help me study."

"You did not," she protested.

"Okay, I didn't."

She narrowed her gaze on him. "I never thought about it

before, but it does seem strange that the only class you ever struggled in was that one."

He shrugged.

"Even way back then, when I thought I was helping you, you were really helping me, weren't you?"

"How did tutoring me help you?"

"It made me feel useful. It helped us become friends." She looked up at him. "I wish Becca had a friend like you."

"She's got something even better—a sister who will do anything for her."

"Unfortunately, I can't make choices for her."

"You're referring to the boyfriend again," he guessed.

Kenna nodded. "I don't know what a seventeen-year-old would want with a girl three years his junior—aside from the obvious—and I refuse to think about that."

"You're not giving your sister enough credit—she's a beautiful, smart and charming young woman."

"When she's not being stupid, stubborn and moody."

He smiled. "Maybe he likes her anyway."

"Think back to when you were seventeen. Did you waste your time with a girl who wouldn't sleep with you?"

"There was one," he remembered. "She was so beautiful, she actually took my breath away. But she made it very clear, very quickly, that I wasn't going to get anywhere with her."

"And that was the end of it," she concluded.

"Actually, no, it was only the beginning." He squeezed her hand. "She became my best friend."

And over the past ten years, he'd never felt as if a single minute of the time he'd spent with her was wasted. A realization that helped him recognize that the next twelve months weren't just the time frame of their marriage but an opportunity to see what the future might hold for both of them together.

Kenna didn't realize she'd fallen asleep until Daniel nudged her awake. She lifted her head from his shoulder just as the doctor stepped through the doors of the surgical wing. She immediately rose to her feet, and Daniel stood with her.

She'd met Dr. Rakem before. She hadn't been impressed by his personality—he was abrupt to the point of rudeness, painfully honest and incredibly blunt. But Kenna didn't want to be his friend. She wanted him to fix her sister's leg.

He gave a brief report on the surgery, most of which she didn't understand. But when he was finished with the technical jargon, he said, "I have every confidence that the surgery was a success."

Kenna shook his hand and thanked him. As the doctor walked away, Daniel put his arms around her and held her close while tears of relief flooded her eyes and spilled onto her cheeks.

She honestly didn't know what she'd do without him in her life. He was her best friend, her confidant, her rock. He was the one person she trusted to always stand by her side, the person who instinctively seemed to know when she needed him, sometimes before she even knew it herself.

So if she sometimes felt stirrings of other emotions, uncomfortable licks of attraction, she could ignore them. Not for anything in the world would she risk their comfortable camaraderie.

Except with each day that passed, it was becoming more and more difficult to believe that their friendship was a boundary. Instead, she was starting to think—to hope—that it could be the foundation of something more.

Julie Marlowe's wedding to Lukas Garrett took place in the bride's hometown of Springfield, Massachusetts.

Most of the Garretts from Charisma had made the trip the day before, but Becca had a follow-up appointment with Dr. Rakem after school on Friday, so Kenna and Daniel caught a flight early Saturday morning. Unfortunately there was a delay in getting the baggage off the plane and then they'd had to wait for a cab at the airport, so they barely had time to check in at the hotel and change their attire before they were racing out the door to the church.

Usually Kenna enjoyed weddings and all of the rituals and traditions associated with them, but as she'd watched Lukas and Julie exchange vows, hearing the heartfelt emotion and sincerity in both of their voices, she couldn't help but feel a pang of envy. Then came their first kiss as husband and wife, and it was a kiss filled with passion and promise for their future together. It was the type of happy beginning she'd always dreamed of when she'd thought she might someday marry for all of the right reasons.

Daniel excused himself from the table three times during the meal that followed to make or return phone calls. As they were seated at a table with both of his brothers and a couple of his cousins, it was too much to hope that no one else had noticed his disappearances.

He missed the bride and groom's first dance and, almost twenty minutes later, still had not returned to the table. She knew he was preoccupied with finalizing some details of his agreement with Josh Slater, and if they were back home in Charisma, she wouldn't have cared if he spent two hours on the phone. But it was undeniably awkward to be seated beside his empty chair at his cousin's wedding because he was AWOL.

"Why is a beautiful woman like you sitting alone?"

She glanced up into the warm hazel eyes of Daniel's cousin Ryan. "Because no one has asked me to dance."

"Then let me rectify that," he said, and offered his hand.

She didn't hesitate to accept his invitation. She'd known Ryan almost as long as she'd known Daniel and had crossed paths with him frequently at various Garrett family events. He was rarely without female companionship, so the fact that he seemed to be alone tonight surprised her.

"You didn't bring a date to the wedding?" she asked.

He shook his head. "I've learned that inviting a woman

to an event like this leads to unrealistic expectations about the relationship."

"What do you consider unrealistic?"

"A second date."

She laughed softly. "You're as bad as Nate, and one of these days you're both going to meet the right women and forget your vow to never get married."

"I never said never," he denied. "But I'm perfectly happy with my life the way it is right now."

"Even with your mother lamenting the fact that she's never going to be a grandmother?"

"Braden and Dana are working on that."

He smoothly moved her to the side to avoid colliding with a young couple who were too wrapped up in one another to care that they weren't alone on the dance floor.

"But if I ever did get married," he continued, "especially to a woman as beautiful as you, you can bet I'd want to be dancing with her rather than tucked in a corner with a phone glued to my ear."

"Daniel's got a lot going on right now," she said in her husband's defense.

"That's no excuse for neglecting a wife of...how long have you been married?"

"Two weeks," she admitted.

Exactly fourteen days, but she didn't want him to know that she was marking the calendar—not because every day was wedded bliss but because she was counting toward the one-year anniversary when she and Daniel would both be free of their pretend marriage.

"And I'm not feeling neglected," she told Ryan, though she couldn't deny that she had been until he'd asked her to dance.

"And maybe I was wrong about my cousin's affections," he allowed, turning Kenna so that she could see her husband striding purposefully toward the dance floor.

Daniel stepped in front of them. "If you don't mind," he

spoke to his cousin through gritted teeth, "I'd like to dance with my wife."

"Of course." Ryan agreed to the request easily, but he held on to Kenna's hand for a moment longer and gave it a subtle squeeze before he released it.

As she moved into her husband's arms, she felt a quick thrill run through her veins. He didn't hold her any closer than Ryan had done, so why was her heart suddenly beating faster? Why was her blood humming?

And what was she supposed to do about this inconvenient attraction she felt to her own husband?

Chapter Six

Daniel didn't know what to make of his own impulsive actions, how to interpret the out-of-character behavior. He'd never been possessive or jealous, and he wondered if the ring on his finger had somehow changed that. Except that explanation was just as uncomfortable as the feelings stirring inside him. Yes, Kenna was his wife, but the circumstances of their marriage didn't warrant his instinctive Neanderthal response to finding her in Ryan's arms any more than logic could change it.

"Are you going to tell me why you look as if you want to punch a wall?" Kenna finally asked him.

"The walls are safe—it's my cousin who should be worried."

"Why?" She sounded genuinely baffled.

"Because he was flirting with you."

"He was *not* flirting with me."

"Why were you dancing with him?"

"Because he asked. Because he felt sorry for me that his idiot cousin was more interested in his phone than his wife."

"I was talking to Josh," he said.

"I figured as much."

"So why are you annoyed about the phone call?"

"Because he felt sorry for me," she said again. "Because it was obvious to him—probably to everyone—that our marriage is a sham."

"I've got a piece of paper that says otherwise."

"The fact that it's legal doesn't make it real," she countered.

"This isn't the first time you've gone to a family wedding with me."

"It's the first time with your ring on my finger."

"What difference does that make?"

She shook her head. "You really don't get it."

"Apparently not," he acknowledged.

"The difference is that there should be a difference… but there isn't."

He'd always appreciated that Kenna didn't tiptoe around issues or sugarcoat the truth. But right now, he didn't have a clue what she was talking about. "Huh?"

She sighed, clearly exasperated. Then she nodded toward the edge of the dance floor. "Look at Matt and Georgia," she suggested. "They've been married for almost a year, but they can hardly keep their hands off one another."

He couldn't deny that the couple were totally wrapped up in one another and oblivious to everyone else.

"And Jack and Kelly," Kenna said. "They exchanged vows more than six months ago *and* they're expecting a baby in only a few weeks, but they're still acting like newlyweds.

"Then there's Lukas and Julie," she continued. "Of course, they *are* newlyweds, but they generate heat just looking at each other.

"You and I, on the other hand? We've been married two weeks and have hardly spent ten minutes in the same room tonight."

He thought he finally got what she was saying. "You think I've been neglecting you?"

"*Everyone* thinks you've been neglecting me."

"Since when do you care what anyone else thinks?"

"Since the 'anyone else' is your family," she said.

As he glanced around, he saw that there were a lot of eyes focused in their direction. Because he and Kenna had been friends for so long, everyone knew who she was. But for most of them, this was the first time they'd seen her as his wife. And she was right—he was treating her the same way he'd always treated her, as if she was his best friend.

Determined to compensate for his apparent neglect—and to answer some of the unspoken questions—he drew Kenna closer, so that her body was intimately aligned with his.

Her breath caught. "What are you doing?"

He lowered his head and her scent, something soft and feminine, teased his nostrils and stirred his blood. "Trying to apologize for being a neglectful husband."

"I doubt two minutes on the dance floor will fool anyone."

He brushed his lips over the shell of her ear. "I think it's a good start."

She shivered, the involuntary response causing her breasts to brush against his chest. Looking down, he found himself staring into the shadow between them. Earlier he'd been too preoccupied admiring her long, shapely legs to notice that the low vee at the front of her dress provided a tantalizing glimpse of cleavage. He was definitely noticing now, and his blood began to pound, hot and heavy, in his veins.

He'd decided he could play the part of the doting husband to satisfy his nosy family; he hadn't expected that just holding Kenna close would wreak havoc on his body. He'd always thought of her as a friend first and a woman second. As a result, he'd sometimes forgotten the woman part—but with her soft, feminine curves pressed against him, he was definitely reminded now.

He remembered the first time he'd looked into her eyes, how mesmerized he'd been to discover they were as clear and blue as the summer sky. And then there were those lips. She hadn't bothered with makeup in high school, but she hadn't needed any artificial enhancement to draw attention to the tempting shape of her mouth. The first time she'd smiled at him, he'd found himself wondering what it would be like to kiss her.

At some point over the past ten years, she'd gone from being a beautiful girl to a stunning woman—and it was only recently that he'd finally noticed the full extent of her transformation.

"I've taken you for granted, haven't I?"

"Probably."

"I don't know that I really thought about what this marriage would mean for you, that you were putting your life on hold for me."

"For my sister," she reminded him.

"Becca was the reason you agreed so readily," he acknowledged. "But you would have done it anyway, because you knew how important this opportunity was to me."

"Maybe."

He just looked at her for a long moment.

"Probably," she acknowledged.

The last notes of the song were fading as she started to pull away. But he wasn't ready to let her go just yet. "People are still watching us."

"I think we've satisfied at least some of their curiosity."

A classic Bob Seger tune had more guests moving toward the dance floor, but Daniel still didn't release her.

"You're probably right," he agreed. "But I have to admit to having some curiosity of my own."

She eyed him warily. "About what?"

"Kissing my wife," he said, then lowered his mouth to hers.

Too late, Daniel remembered the saying about curiosity killing the cat.

For just a moment, she held herself completely still, not moving, not even breathing. Obviously she hadn't anticipated his move and didn't know how—or if—to respond. But then her lips softened beneath his, and in the very instant that Kenna began to kiss him back, he knew that one kiss wouldn't be nearly enough. What he'd accepted as a simple and innocent curiosity was immediately swept away on the wave of desire that flooded his system. He thought he'd wanted only to kiss her; now he only wanted.

He drew her closer, wanting to feel the press of her body against his. She didn't resist. In fact, she all but melted against him. And when he touched his tongue to her lips, they parted willingly to grant him entry. He dipped inside, testing, tasting. She responded eagerly, her tongue dancing and dallying with his.

His hand slid up her back, tracing the ridges of her spine through the thin fabric of her dress. His fingers sifted through the silky strands of hair to cup the back of her head as his mouth continued to plunder hers and his mind struggled to make sense of this new development.

After more than ten years of being just friends, he was as shocked as he was aroused by this abrupt shift in his feelings. Or maybe it wasn't so abrupt. Maybe the attraction had always been there, simmering beneath the surface but deliberately ignored.

Certainly he'd noticed her the first day she arrived at Hillfield. Partly because she was new, and new kids were a rarity, especially in the upper grades. But mostly because she was female and hot and he'd been sixteen years old—a hormonally driven age when no one with breasts had been overlooked.

His friends had noticed her, too. As unassuming as she

tried to be, there was no way she could walk through the halls unseen. But she did a pretty good job of freezing everyone out and shooting down awkward advances.

For the first few days, Daniel had mostly just watched her. But when Mr. Taylor had put them together as lab partners, he'd finally had a legitimate excuse to talk to her. He'd sensed that she was more wary than aloof, and he decided to bide his time before making a move.

The day he'd finally managed to convince her to go out with him for pizza, he'd thought about trying to steal a kiss. But fate—in the form of Blake Mackie—had intervened, and he lost his chance.

Then they became friends, and he'd never had a female friend before. Aside from the fact that talking to a girl without mentally calculating the odds of getting her naked was a novelty, he found that he could talk to Kenna about things he didn't talk to his male friends—or anyone else—about. After a while, it was just too weird to think about kissing her. In his mind, she had transitioned from a potential girlfriend to a real friend, which meant not only that he couldn't make a move on her, but he wouldn't let any of his friends, either.

Right now, however, he wasn't thinking about any of that old history. He was thinking only about the softness of her lips, the sweetness of her mouth and the unexpected passion of her response.

He didn't want to stop kissing her, except maybe long enough to peel away the dress she was wearing so that he could kiss her all over—down the smooth column of her throat, along the sexy slope of her shoulders, over the sweet curve of her breasts. He wanted to lick her nipples with his tongue and make her gasp, then suckle deeply and hear her moan. He wanted to part those mile-long legs and bury himself deep inside her; he wanted her arching and straining to meet him, thrust for thrust.

And the wanting was so vivid and real, he almost forgot

they were at his cousin's wedding, still standing on the edge of the dance floor as people moved around them.

Thankfully they were staying in the same hotel in which the reception was being held, which meant they could be in their room in about three minutes and naked in less than half that time again. And the prospect of getting naked with Kenna was irresistible.

He eased his mouth from hers but continued to hold her close. "Why don't we take this upstairs?"

She looked up at him, those beautiful blue eyes dark and unfocused, proof that she was as turned on right now as he was. She touched her tongue to her bottom lip. "Upstairs?"

"We have a king-size bed on the tenth floor," he reminded her.

Before she could respond to that, his phone vibrated inside his jacket pocket.

Kenna could feel the silent ringing of his cell against her hip. It was like a soundless alarm, awakening her from an erotic dream, and she was grateful for the interruption. Because while being in Daniel's arms had felt like heaven, she couldn't expect one kiss—as fabulous as it was—to exorcise all of her demons. And the prospect of sharing more than one kiss was both tempting and terrifying.

Tempting because she wanted to explore the feelings he stirred inside her, and terrifying because she was afraid that going any further would lead only to disappointment and heartache.

Daniel knew her better than anyone else in the world, and she trusted him more than she trusted anyone else. But there were still things he didn't know about her, secrets she hadn't shared with anyone and that she didn't intend to reveal even to the man who was now her husband. Not because of any fault on his part, but because she wasn't strong enough or brave enough to lay her soul bare. And so she could want and wonder about making love with Daniel Garrett until the sun came up, but it wasn't going to happen outside of her fantasies.

His phone hummed again.

She drew in a deep breath and, silently praying that her wobbly knees would support her, took a step back, out of his arms. "You should get that."

"I won't be long," he promised.

"It's okay. I have to—" Several options raced through her scrambled brain: go to the ladies' room, get a drink, jump off a bridge—preferably into a very cold lake—and definitely *not* think about the fact that locking lips with her best friend had totally shaken her world, but she finally seized upon "—go to the ladies' room."

He nodded, his phone already in his hand, and she made her escape.

She found the nearest facility and slipped inside, hopeful for a quiet, dark corner where she could catch her breath and get her suddenly rampant hormones under control.

What she found instead was the bride and one of her sisters-in-law hanging out in the lounge area. Any hope that she might be able to sneak past and hide in a stall was dashed when Jackson's wife—settled on one end of a velvet-covered settee and rubbing her swollen belly—caught her eye.

"I didn't have a chance to say more than a quick 'hi' when you passed through the receiving line," Kelly said, "but you're Daniel's wife, aren't you?"

Kenna managed a smile as she nodded. "Yes, I am."

"Congratulations." The bride offered her hand. "I hear you surprised the whole family with the Vegas elopement."

"*Surprised* is probably an understatement," Kenna confided. "But we wanted to be married more than we wanted a wedding." Then, realizing that she may have offended the bride, she hastened to add, "Although your wedding today was beautiful."

Julie's chuckle proved she wasn't insulted by the comment. "Lukas didn't want a big wedding, either."

"Lukas would have got married in the middle of a three-ring circus if it was what you wanted," Kelly interjected.

The slow smile that curved the bride's lips confirmed she knew this was true. "But it wouldn't have been his first choice," she clarified. "And while all I wanted was to become Mrs. Lukas Garrett, there was no way my mother was going to let me get married without all the bells and whistles, especially when I'd already committed the unforgivable sin of having a baby before she even knew that I was pregnant."

"I don't think I heard that part of the story," Kenna admitted, her curiosity piqued.

"Another time," the bride said, as her other sister-in-law—Matthew's wife—lowered herself onto the seat beside Kelly.

"Are you okay?" Julie asked.

Georgia nodded. "My stomach's just been a little unsettled lately."

The expectant mother looked wary. "Are you contagious?"

"Maybe I should have asked you that question a few months back."

"You're pregnant," Kelly immediately realized.

She nodded again, and the confirmation was met with squeals of joy and hugs all around.

"Why didn't you say anything?"

"How far along are you?"

"Do the kids know?"

"I didn't say anything," Georgia explained, when they finally let her speak, "because we wanted to wait a little while longer before sharing the news. I'm only about eight weeks along, and no, the kids don't know yet."

"Did you have morning sickness with your other pregnancies?" Julie asked.

"With the twins, but not with Pippa."

"Maybe that means you're having another boy," Kelly said.

"Or another set of twins," Julie suggested.

"Bite your tongue," Georgia admonished.

The bride grinned unrepentantly.

"I thought morning sickness only happened in the morning," Kenna said.

"Unfortunately not," Georgia said. "In fact, I'm usually fine in the morning and it's not until later in the day that the nausea strikes." She opened her purse to take out a package of dry crackers and a bottle of water.

"I'm in awe," Julie said. "I feel like I'm over my head with Caden sometimes, and you have twins just finishing kindergarten, a not-yet-two-year-old and now another baby on the way."

"We thought four was a good number," Georgia said. "I know Matt couldn't possibly love Quinn and Shane and Pippa any more than he already does—and his eagerness to formally adopt them and share his name proved that to me. But I wanted to have a baby with him, to share the connection of a biological child.

"Of course, we were thinking we would wait until Pippa was a couple of years older, but fate obviously had other ideas."

"I want to have a baby with Lukas," Julie confided. "I know Caden's not even a year old and we've only been married a few hours, but I want a baby with my husband."

"Lukas would be a great father," Kelly assured her.

"He already is," the bride said, before turning to Kenna to ask, "How about you?"

"Me?" she squeaked, taken aback by the shift of the conversation in her direction.

"I know you've only been married a couple of weeks," Julie said. "But have you and Daniel talked about having kids?"

She shook her head, immediately and vehemently.

The other women chuckled.

"Jackson and I planned to wait, too," Kelly told her, continuing to rub gentle circles over her belly. "But things don't always work out the way we plan."

The truth was, Kenna and Daniel had no plans for kids at all. Their only plan was a quiet and civilized divorce following their one-year anniversary.

Two weeks down, only fifty more to go.

"You know the saying 'life is what happens when you're making other plans'?" Georgia asked.

At Kenna's nod, she continued, "My twist on that would be 'kids are what happen when they're not anywhere in your plans.'"

"I can attest to that," Kelly agreed. "Twice now."

"Caden was an unexpected surprise, too," Julie chimed in.

Kenna smiled and ignored the longing that tugged at her heart. As much as she wanted a child of her own someday, she knew the chances of her and Daniel having a baby together were somewhere between nil and zero. Because babies weren't born of platonic relationships.

And one mind-numbing kiss on the dance floor aside, she didn't see the nature of their relationship changing anytime soon.

Daniel ended his phone call and surveyed the reception area, looking for Kenna. Josh had given him some promising news and he was eager to share it with her.

For the past ten years, she'd been the first person he wanted to call when he had good news, the one person he knew would always be in his corner when it seemed as if no one else was, and the only woman he'd considered proposing marriage to when he'd decided that was what he had to do. In fact, he hadn't really considered marriage an option until he'd considered marriage to Kenna. Which made him wonder if he'd really married her because he wanted to get his hands on the money…or because he wanted to get his hands on Kenna.

But if they took that next step and their relationship shifted from friendship to intimacy, would that jeopardize everything they shared? And was he willing to take the chance that he might lose her as a friend because he was suddenly feeling a lot more than friendly?

But why did it have to be one or the other? Why couldn't they be friends *and* lovers?

The logical part of his brain immediately jumped all over that question, warning that if he took Kenna to his bed, they might never be able to go back to being just friends again. And as much as he was having trouble focusing on anything but getting her naked, he had to wonder what they'd do if the actual event turned out to be awkward or uncomfortable.

Yeah, the kiss they'd shared had been off the charts, but he knew from experience that didn't necessarily translate into compatibility in the bedroom.

Then she walked back into the room, and he felt something move inside him. It was more than just a stirring low in his belly—it was a tug on his heart.

"What's up with Josh?" Kenna asked, when she joined him by the bar.

"He had a meeting with Ren this afternoon, and while no deal has been made, Ren wants to continue discussions."

She knew that Ren was stock car driver Lorenzo D'Alesio. According to countless posts on his fan site, he was sexy and charismatic and incredibly talented. Daniel and Josh both believed he was also frustrated by the reality of being the third driver on a team that routinely entered only two cars in a race. Unfortunately, that team was owned by his father, so the odds of luring him away weren't exactly favorable.

"That's great news," Kenna said. "He wouldn't be talking to you if he wasn't at least a little bit interested."

Daniel nodded. "But he's still a long shot."

Kenna hoped it was one that would pay off. Daniel had

poured his heart and soul—not to mention nearly every penny of the trust fund that had been the motivating factor of their marriage—into Garrett/Slater Racing, and she wanted it to be a success for him.

She knew that some people—even Daniel's brothers—thought his desire to own a race team was a whim, but Kenna knew better. Her husband's love affair with stock cars dated back to his early teens, when Josh invited him to Daytona to watch his uncle race, and this was a dream that they'd both been working toward for years.

She was proud that he had the courage and determination to pursue it, and just a little envious. While her own dreams were much simpler, she didn't have the first clue about how to make them happen.

She lifted a hand, trying to stifle a yawn, but Daniel caught the movement out of the corner of his eye.

"It's been a long week for you," he noted.

She nodded. Exams had just finished and needed to be marked, then final grades had to be submitted. And the upcoming week would be nearly as busy, with numerous staff meetings to tie up loose ends and start planning for the next year. On top of all that, because it was difficult for Becca to get on and off the bus with her crutches, Kenna had been chauffeuring her sister around whenever Sue Ellen was working.

Daniel reached for her hand and twined their fingers together. "Ready to call it a night?"

She was tired enough to happily slip between the sheets of the big bed to sleep. Unfortunately, her body was still so revved from his kiss that she knew sleep would be impossible. But if he wanted to slide between those sheets with her—

She mentally severed the thought. Taking the next step with Daniel was…if not impossible, at least inadvisable.

"I'm ready," she agreed. "But I don't want to drag you away from the party."

"Then I'll drag you," he said, leading her to the elevator.

The doors to the car opened immediately, and she stepped inside. When he punched the button for the tenth floor, she considered that she might have read too much into a simple question. Maybe he was just as tired as she was and had no expectation of anything except to fall into bed and sleep. Because he didn't say anything to her when the doors closed. He didn't try to kiss her. He didn't even touch her.

But there was an undeniable sizzle in the air, an electricity that danced over her skin and made her body hum.

She forced herself to keep breathing, to focus on the display above the door that tracked the elevator's progress toward their destination and ignore the heat pulsing through her veins.

…2…

Ignore the fact that there was only one bed in their room.

…3…

The desk clerk who checked them in had happily informed them that they'd been upgraded from a standard room with two double beds to a deluxe with a king-size and whirlpool tub.

…4…5…

Neither of them had given it much thought at the time, because they'd been focused on getting to the church.

…6…

Now, however, it was all Kenna could think about.

…7…

Two people.

…8…

One bed.

…9…

One king-size dilemma.

Ding.

The elevator chimed to signal its arrival. With a soft whoosh, the doors parted, and Daniel gestured for her to exit.

She stepped out into the hall and automatically headed toward Room 1064, still with no idea where she was going.

Chapter Seven

Kenna's heart was pounding so loudly, she was amazed that Daniel couldn't hear it. When they got to their door, he slipped his key card into the slot, and the light blinked green.

Was that some kind of subliminal message? Did green mean she was supposed to go for it? Or was she looking for signs where there were none to be found?

Daniel followed her into the room, and the door closed with a quiet click that made her jolt.

He shrugged out of his jacket and draped it over the back of a chair, then loosened the knot of the tie at his throat. He was one of those guys who wore a suit as easily and comfortably as if he'd been born in it, and she hadn't been oblivious to the covetous female glances sent in his direction.

It had always been that way. There was something about Daniel that set him apart, even in a room filled with handsome men. She didn't know if it was the warmth of his eyes, the quickness of his smile or something less tangible, but women had always been drawn to him.

Even she hadn't been immune, though she'd learned to

fake it well enough to convince both of them otherwise. But she didn't think she could fake it anymore. Not after that kiss.

And why should she pretend, when that had never really worked out for her before? She'd exaggerated the depth of her feelings for Harrison because she'd thought that if she told herself she loved him, she might actually fall in love with him. But while his kisses and his touches had continued to leave her cold, it seemed as though Daniel only had to look at her and she felt as if she was burning up inside.

"What are you thinking?"

She turned to find him looking at her now, and warmth immediately spread through her veins, pooled at her center.

"I'm having trouble forming any coherent thoughts at all," she admitted.

"Thinking is highly overrated anyway," he said, and lowered his head to kiss her again.

She wasn't caught off guard this time. At least not completely. And still, she was unprepared for the effect his kiss had on her. It was a gentle brush of his lips against hers, more coaxing than demanding, and she was more than willing to be coaxed. Even while questions and concerns continued to swirl through her mind, her body was pressing against his, eager for more.

No one else's kisses had ever made her feel so much—or want so much more. The array of emotions he managed to elicit from just the touch of his mouth to hers was almost overwhelming. His tongue stroked hers—teasing and tempting—as his hands skimmed up her torso, brushing the sides of her breasts and causing goose bumps to dance over her skin. Then his thumbs grazed her nipples, and her knees actually trembled.

She let her hands move over him, absorbing the strength and heat of his muscles through the fabric of his shirt. He had a lot of muscles for a guy who spent so many hours behind a desk every day. And as her fingers roamed over various ridges and contours, she knew that she wanted every inch of that hard, strong body pressed against her.

She tugged his shirt out of the waistband of his pants as he lifted his mouth from hers to nip gently at her chin, nibble on her ear, then trail kisses down her throat. He pushed the skinny straps of her dress over her shoulders, then pressed his mouth to the skin he'd exposed. His tongue traced the ridge of her collarbone, then continued down the center of her breastbone, and finally dipped into the hollow between her breasts.

She'd always had issues with physical intimacy, so when Daniel tugged the bodice of her dress down, she held her breath, waiting for the chill to steal over her, for the rigidity to set into her bones.

He seemed to sense her tension, and although he didn't deviate from his course, his mouth gentled. His lips feathered lightly over her skin, the barest hint of a caress that nevertheless reached into the deepest part of her, escalating her desire so there was no room for anything else. That quickly, the last of her tension drained away, leaving her weak and wanting.

And when he took the exposed nipple in his mouth, she felt nothing but heat and hunger. When his tongue swirled around the already taut peak, she gasped at the exquisite sensations that arrowed toward her core.

She longed to feel his bare skin against hers, to connect intimately with him without any barriers between them. The need was strong and real and unlike anything she'd ever experienced before. Because being with Daniel made her forget all of her usual doubts and insecurities. In his arms, she felt safe, secure, cherished.

Despite his occasional and deliberately suggestive comments, he wasn't just some guy looking to score with any willing woman. He was a friend—her best friend. The one person she'd always been able to count on; the only person who'd never let her down.

And she knew that he never would. If they made love, he would make sure that she enjoyed every minute of it, that she would have absolutely no regrets when it was over. In light of her own limited and disappointing experiences, she wasn't half as confident that she could do the same for him.

He'd just located the zipper at the back of her dress when a knock sounded. He froze, the pull halfway down, and swore under his breath.

The knock sounded again, followed by a muffled announcement through the door. "Room Service."

"Don't move," he said, and pressed a quick, hard kiss to Kenna's lips before stepping closer to the door. "We didn't order any room service."

"Compliments of David and Jane Garrett."

She tugged at the bodice of her dress to ensure everything was covered and he finally, reluctantly, opened the door.

The waiter wheeled in a cart. "Where would you like it set up, sir?"

"Just leave it right there." Daniel pressed some bills into the man's hand and nudged him out the door again.

Kenna tried to catch her breath as she surveyed the contents of the tray: a bottle of champagne in a silver bucket of ice, two long-stemmed crystal flutes, a handful of short-stemmed pink sweetheart roses in a bowl and a plate of plump, juicy strawberries elaborately decorated with white and dark chocolate so it looked as if they were wearing tuxedo jackets.

She picked up the card.

Daniel & Kenna,
Since you haven't yet had a proper wedding or a honeymoon, we wanted to give you at least one night of romance.
Love Mom & Dad
xoxo

The signature line brought tears to her eyes and made her realize how dangerously close she'd come to making a very big mistake.

Because she already loved his family as much as she loved Daniel, and she knew that if they blurred the lines of their relationship—and mixing sex with their friendship was a surefire way to blur the lines—she might start to blur the lines of her relationship with his family, too. Then she might start thinking this marriage was real and dreaming of a future for them together, and that definitely wasn't part of their plan.

Daniel, apparently oblivious to the emotional battle raging inside her, lifted the bottle from the ice bucket and examined the label. "Champagne?"

She shook her head.

His gaze narrowed. "What's wrong?"

"Don't you feel the least bit guilty about lying to your family?"

"I don't feel good about it, but we both agreed it was the only solution," he reminded her.

She nodded, because he was right. They'd both agreed to this twelve-month marriage, and they weren't even through the first month of it yet. It was easy, when they were each busy with their own lives, to pretend that nothing had changed. But they were husband and wife now, their lives inextricably entwined.

Until recently, she'd been so focused on Becca's surgery that she hadn't let herself think very far beyond that. Now that the surgery was over and her sister was finally starting on the road to recovery, the next eleven and a half months loomed ominously and endlessly ahead, filled with holidays and events that she and Daniel would be expected to attend together, as husbands and wives were wont to do.

She didn't think she could keep up the charade through the holidays, spending time with his family, feeling as if she was part of his family and desperately wishing that she really was. She knew she wouldn't be able to do it unless she and Daniel each remained clear about their roles in, and the expiration date of, this pretend marriage.

"We can't do this," she told him now.

He dropped the bottle back into the ice. "I assume you're not talking about the champagne."

"I'm not talking about the champagne," she confirmed. "You're my best friend in the whole world, Daniel. I'm not going to risk that for the sake of a quick thrill between the sheets."

He snaked an arm around her waist and pulled her close. "I promise you, it won't be quick."

His response, so typically and arrogantly male, made her smile. But she still took a step back, needing distance between them to ensure that she didn't fall back into his arms. "I'm trying to be logical here."

"Not everything is logical."

She nodded, unable to deny it when her feelings for him were proof enough of the point. But she still wasn't willing to jeopardize her heart for momentary physical satisfaction.

"Do you love me, Daniel?"

"Yes."

His response was immediate and unequivocal, which was when she realized she'd asked the wrong question. "But are you *in* love with me?"

He eyed her warily. "No one means as much to me as you do."

"I feel the same way," she assured him. "And we both know this isn't a till-death-do-us-part marriage—it's a till-we-both-get-what-we-want marriage, and if we fall into bed together—"

"That would certainly be what *I* want," he told her.

Right now, it was what she wanted, too. And this kind of wanting, the desperate, achy need that had everything inside her churned up, was as scary as it was unfamiliar.

"And after?" she prompted.

He sighed. "You're determined to analyze this to death, aren't you?"

"I don't want either of us to have regrets."

"There's something between us, Kenna. Maybe it's unexpected and inconvenient, but it's not going to go away just because you want it to."

"What's between us is a decade of friendship and some unexpected sparks as a result of the fact that we've been living in close proximity for the past two weeks. And being a guy, you assumed that the ring on my finger was a shortcut to getting me into bed."

He frowned at that. "I didn't assume anything except that you wanted me as much as I wanted you."

"You don't want me, Daniel. You want sex."

"I want sex with *you*."

"Because we're married and you're too honorable to cheat, even on a temporary wife. The two weeks since our wedding is probably the longest you've gone without sex since high school."

"Actually, it's been more than six months."

"Six months?"

"Why do you sound so surprised? You know I haven't been seeing anyone."

She shrugged. "I guess I just didn't figure you had to be dating a woman to sleep with her."

"There was a time when you would have been right," he admitted. "But at some point over the past few years, I started wanting more than sex for the sake of sex."

"I'm stunned...and impressed," she told him.

"How long has it been since you've had sex?" he challenged.

She felt her cheeks flush. "Longer than you."

"Maybe that's part of the reason for the sparks. And maybe we'd both feel a lot better if—"

"No."

His brows lifted. "You didn't let me finish."

"I could see where you were going with that completely self-serving argument."

"I wasn't being self-serving but offering my services."

"No," she said again.

"You really think we can just ignore the attraction?"

"Yes, I do," she said.

He stepped closer, brushed his fingertips over the pulse point fluttering below her ear. His lips curved. "Really?"

She swatted his hand away. "I'm going to take a shower."

"Want me to wash your back?"

Her only response was to close and lock the bathroom door.

He found the remote control and turned on the TV. He needed to focus on something other than the sound of water running and the knowledge that Kenna was naked and wet on the other side of a door secured by a flimsy lock that he could probably open in two seconds. Because along with the thoughts *naked* and *wet* came a whole kaleidoscope of incredibly vivid and arousing mental images.

He wondered if there was something lacking in his moral character that he didn't even feel guilty for having prurient fantasies about his best friend. Or maybe Kenna was right—maybe the fact that they'd been living in close proximity was messing with his mind as well as his libido. Or maybe he was only just acknowledging feelings that he'd denied for too long.

He scrolled through the channels until he found a West Coast baseball game on one of the sports channels. Since it was there, he opened the bottle of champagne and took the plate of strawberries over to the chair. He popped one of the berries into his mouth and washed it down with a mouthful of the bubbly wine. It probably wasn't what his parents had in mind when they'd sent the tray to their room, but Daniel didn't see any point in letting it go to waste.

And then, because the gift had been for both of them, he set a couple of strawberries aside on a napkin and poured a glass of champagne for Kenna, too.

He tried to focus on the game, but when he heard the water shut off, his attention wandered behind that closed door again. It was easy to imagine her tugging a towel from the rack…rubbing it over her body…wiping away all traces of moisture from the slick, glistening skin of her shoulders… her arms…her breasts…. He could picture the towel stroking down her torso…over the curve of her hip…between her thighs….

He picked up his glass and gulped down another mouthful of champagne.

A few minutes later, he heard the hair dryer start up, and he punched up the volume on the television.

When she finally came out of the bathroom, she was dressed in her pajamas—a pair of silky red boxer-style shorts and an old MIT T-shirt. He did a double take.

"Is that my shirt?"

"It was," she corrected. "Now it's mine."

"You stole it out of my closet?"

"No. Out of your laundry basket…six years ago."

"Six *years* ago?" he echoed.

She nodded. "The weekend I came to Boston to visit you."

"Why?"

"Because I missed you," she admitted.

He considered telling her that she could have *him* wrapped around her instead of his old shirt, but it probably wasn't smart to go down that road again, not while the taste of her kiss still lingered on his lips and his desire for her continued to pulse in his blood. And especially not when she'd made it clear that anything more than the few kisses they'd already shared wasn't ever going to happen.

He might not like her decision or completely agree with the rationale, but he respected that it was her choice. And maybe she was right. Maybe his desire was more about how long it had been since he'd had sex than it was about wanting Kenna. But looking at her now, sitting cross-legged on top of the covers in those ridiculous pj's with her face bare of makeup and a smudge of chocolate on her lower lip from the strawberry she held in one hand, the surge of lust through his system suggested otherwise.

Yeah, it had been a long time since he'd had sex, but right now, he didn't want anyone but her.

When the ball game went into extra innings, Kenna returned to the bathroom to brush her teeth. Then she slipped under the covers of the bed, taking the side farther away from the chair where he was sitting.

"You don't have to cling to the edge of the mattress," he told her. "I'll sleep in this chair."

"You won't be comfortable in that," she protested.

"I've slept in worse places." And it would be infinitely more comfortable than the prospect of sharing a bed with her and not being able to touch her.

"The bed's big enough that I'm sure neither of us will even notice the other one is in it," she said, without releasing her grip on the edge.

He didn't believe that for a second. Yes, the bed was big, but every inch of his body was so closely attuned to hers now that he knew if she so much as shifted her head on her pillow, he'd notice. If he wanted to get any shut-eye, the chair was his best option.

He did fall asleep where he was, but his plans to stay in the chair through the night didn't last. He woke at 2:00 a.m., then again at two-thirty, and at three-twenty. Finally, around four o'clock, he crawled into bed with his wife.

There had been a time—and not too long ago—when the idea of settling down with one woman would have made him break out in hives. But being married to Kenna didn't feel like settling at all. Somehow, it just felt right.

* * *

He woke up several hours later with Kenna in his arms.

He had no idea how she got there. Even at 4:00 a.m., she'd been on the far side of the bed, clinging to the edge of the mattress when he'd finally eased beneath the covers on the opposite side. But sometime during the night, they'd moved toward one another.

Actually, he realized with surprise and amusement, he hadn't moved at all. He was still clearly on his side of the bed while hers was empty. Her one knee was between his, and his arm was around her, his hand splayed on her back beneath the hem of her/his T-shirt.

Through the thin cotton of that old shirt, he could see the pointy outline of her nipples, and his mouth went dry. As if of its own volition, his hand slid upward, stroking the smooth bare skin of her back. She murmured something indecipherable and snuggled closer to him. The action brought their bodies more fully into contact, and a certain part of his anatomy, known for being much more awake in the morning than the rest of him, was standing at attention.

Her head was against his shoulder, and he could feel the soft whisper of her breath against his throat as she exhaled. The slow and regular rhythm of her breathing confirmed that she was still asleep, and he wondered if it was possible to extricate himself without waking her. Not that he wanted to give up the undeniable pleasure of her soft curves pressed against him, but after his repeated assurances that he would sleep in the chair, he didn't know what she'd think if she woke up and found herself plastered against him.

He removed his hand from inside her shirt first, albeit with great reluctance. She didn't stir. He held his breath for another half a minute, then he shifted his top leg, just a fraction. The soft, sharp intake of her breath warned him that she'd awakened.

"Good morning," he said softly.

She tilted her head to look at him, her deep blue eyes

clouded with sleep and an array of emotions he couldn't begin to decipher. "I thought you were going to sleep in the chair."

"I tried. But it wasn't very comfortable."

She just nodded.

"I did, however, stay on my side of the bed."

She opened her mouth as if to argue the point, then closed it again when she realized he was speaking the truth—that *she* was snuggled up to *him* on his side of the bed.

"Sorry." She tried to scoot away, but he tightened his arm before she could do so. "I'm used to sleeping in the middle."

"No need to apologize or explain," he assured. "I've never objected to waking up with a sexy woman in my arms."

"I'm not a sexy woman—I'm your temporary wife."

He smiled at that. "You're my incredibly sexy and undeniably argumentative wife."

"And I'm hungry," she told him.

He suspected she wasn't nearly as hungry as she was anxious to get out of the bed where they were intimately entwined, but he followed her lead. "I suppose that's your way of telling me that you want to get up so we can go for breakfast?"

"Breakfast would be good."

"Give me ten minutes to shower."

Chapter Eight

Kenna breathed a sigh of relief when Daniel slipped out of bed and disappeared into the bathroom. For just a minute there, she'd been tempted to ignore all of the reasons and logic she'd enumerated the night before and throw herself into his arms.

Except that she'd already been in his arms. And waking up in the warm shelter of his embrace had been... indescribable. During those moments when she'd balanced on the edge between asleep and awake, she'd felt safe and warm and normal. For a few seconds before reality intruded, she hadn't wanted to be anywhere else but exactly where she was.

Then she remembered that their marriage was only a temporary arrangement, and that allowing herself to believe differently, if only for a few seconds, could ruin everything. She'd meant what she'd said to him the night they got married—she didn't want their marriage to ruin their friendship. What she didn't tell him was that she was afraid of so much more than losing her best friend—she was afraid that she would never have a normal relationship with any man because of the emotional scars she still carried from high school.

Kenna and Libby had known each other since sixth grade, but she hadn't seen her friend at all since she'd transferred to Hillfield. However, she knew that Libby always worked Friday afternoons at Mossimo's, so when she said goodbye to Daniel, she went back to the kitchen and found her friend up to her elbows in sudsy water, scrubbing pots and pans and pizza trays.

"Hey, Libby."

Her friend looked up for half a second before she resumed her scrubbing. "What are you doing here?"

"I haven't seen you in a while. I wanted to say 'hi.'"

"Where's your boyfriend?"

The fierceness in her tone surprised Kenna as much as the question. "What?"

"Blake said you came in here with some guy."

Blake was Libby's brother, older by almost two years. He hadn't paid much attention to his sister or any of her friends when they were kids, but when Kenna's body started to develop curves, right around her thirteenth birthday, he'd taken notice. She wanted to believe he was mostly harmless, but she didn't like the way he looked at her, and his crude language made her uncomfortable.

"So Blake saw me come in with some guy and he raced back here to tell you?"

Libby shrugged. "He was pissed because you've never given him the time of day."

"Aside from the fact that I don't date, going out with your brother would be a little too weird."

"Is that really why—or were you just waiting for someone better, maybe someone richer, to come along?"

"I can't believe you would even ask that."

"I can't believe you abandoned all your friends to go

to Hillfield." Libby spit out the name of the school as if it was distasteful.

"I'm sorry you see it that way."

"That's the way it is."

Kenna didn't argue, because it was obvious that Libby wouldn't listen to her. "I'll see you around," she said, and headed out the back door, as she usually did after visiting Libby in the kitchen.

She jolted when she found Blake waiting for her.

"Who is he?" he demanded.

She sighed. "Just a guy I know from school."

"So he's rich."

"I'm not dating him, Blake."

"Did he buy your dinner?"

"It was just a pizza." She started to walk past him, but he grabbed her arm, his fingers digging into her flesh, making her wince. "Ow. Stop it, Blake."

"Stop it?" He pushed her up against the wall, and pressed against her. "I bet you don't tell him to stop it."

What had begun as mild irritation quickly escalated to genuine fear as she realized he wasn't just bigger and stronger, but completely irrational. "It's not like that."

"You expect me to believe that you're not screwing him?"

At another time, she might have told him it was none of his business, but right now, fear was giving way to panic. She pushed against his chest, but she couldn't move him. And she couldn't ignore the hard bulge at the front of his pants, grinding against her. "No, I'm not screwing him."

"I don't believe you."

The pizza she'd eaten churned in her stomach, threatened to rise up. "Blake, please—"

He crushed his mouth against hers so hard her head rapped back against the brick, making her see stars. Then his tongue was in her mouth, so deep she nearly gagged, and his hands were on her breasts, squeezing hard.

She'd never seen him like this. His eyes were wild and un-

focused, and she knew he had something in his system that was fueling his meanness and his fury. He continued to grind against her, as his hands moved from her breasts to her skirt, then beneath. She struggled against him, but to no avail. He yanked her panties down to her knees and, in that moment, she was certain he would rape her if she didn't get away.

He shifted to unfasten his jeans, and she knew this might be her only chance. She brought up her knee and slammed it into his groin as hard as she could. He staggered back two steps before dropping to the ground, swearing.

She didn't wait to see if he was okay. She didn't care. She turned and ran—and collided with Daniel Garrett.

His gaze skimmed over her, taking in her swollen mouth and torn shirt, then shifted to Blake, still gasping and swearing on the ground.

"Are you okay?"

The gentleness of his tone made her want to cry, but she nodded. "What— Why are you still here?"

"You forgot your leftover pizza," he said.

"Oh." She accepted the take-out container he offered. She was suddenly cold and shaky, and it was an effort to keep her teeth from chattering. "Thanks."

"Can I give you a ride home now?"

She nodded again, then took an instinctive step back when she saw that Blake had managed to stagger to his feet.

Daniel started toward him, but she reached for his arm. "Don't. P-please. Just let it go."

He touched a gentle finger to her puffy lip. "I'm sorry— I can't do that."

In half a dozen strides, he was beside Blake, holding him by the front of the shirt. He kept his voice low enough that she couldn't hear what he said, but she had no trouble hearing Blake's crude reply.

Daniel's response was a quick and powerful uppercut to the jaw that knocked Blake to the ground again.

Then he calmly led her back to his car and drove her home.

The apartment was empty, because her mother was at work and Becca was at after-school day care. He dampened a cloth and carefully dabbed at her bloody lip, and he talked to her, about all kinds of things that had nothing to do with what had happened at the restaurant. He didn't seem to care that it was an entirely one-sided conversation. He just talked and talked until she finally stopped shaking. And he stayed with her until her mother got home.

Was it any wonder she felt safe with him, secure in his arms without even a hint of the familiar panic rearing its ugly head, as it often did at the most inopportune times?

She'd seen a counselor, had been reassured that all of her feelings were perfectly normal and that she would eventually overcome her struggles with physical intimacy. But more than ten years later, Kenna continued to find it difficult to open up and share her body.

She wanted that intimacy, she wanted to be normal, but there were still occasions when a man's touch made her freeze up. Not every time, but often enough that she'd started to expect it, and to dread it. She hated that feeling of vulnerability, because along with the powerlessness came panic. Sometimes she managed to talk herself through it, and sometimes she didn't.

She'd felt none of that helplessness or fear with Daniel the night before. She'd felt nothing but pleasure—sometimes shockingly fierce and intense, but still only pleasure. Even when she'd registered the press of his erection against her belly, she hadn't felt afraid, only aroused. She'd wanted to tear away their clothes and feel the hard length of him pushing deep inside her.

And when she'd awakened in his arms, with the evidence of his arousal between them, her nipples had pebbled and she'd experienced an unmistakable throbbing between her thighs, a desperate yearning unlike anything she'd ever known before.

The realization caused a thought to stir along with her hormones: Was it possible that Daniel might be the man who could help her overcome her residual fears and move forward with her life?

She knew that having sex with her husband wouldn't change any of the terms of their agreement. He'd been clear from the start that he didn't want a permanent wife. As he'd explained it to her, he had to get married to satisfy the terms of the trust, but he didn't have the time or the emotional energy to put into a real relationship while he was focused on making Garrett/Slater Racing a legitimate contender on the stock car circuit. Which was why he believed she was the perfect candidate for his plan.

His proposal might not have been romantic, but at least it was honest. She wasn't bothered by his statement that he didn't want to be tied down, because she had no interest in tying him down. She only wanted to make sure that Becca would have the surgery and rehab she needed to walk normally again.

But now she wanted something more. She wanted to be his wife in every sense of the word for the duration of their agreement—or at least for as long as he wanted her.

She knew that sharing physical intimacy wouldn't change anything for them—but it could change *everything* for her. She didn't want to spend the rest of her life alone, but she'd had trouble opening up with other men and she was weary of being dismissed as clumsy or frigid or simply not worth the effort.

Daniel could be the partner who made her feel safe enough to exorcise those old demons. And if she could learn to enjoy true physical intimacy, to fully and freely participate in the act of lovemaking, maybe she would be able to open up her heart and actually fall in love. And then she could finally put her past in the past and move forward with her life.

Which meant that she had to figure out how to seduce her husband.

It wasn't until Daniel got out of the shower that he realized he had nothing to put on. But Kenna had seen him in a towel before, and while this one wasn't oversize like the ones he had in his bathroom at home, he figured it covered him adequately enough for the brief trek back into the bedroom to dig some clothes out of his bag.

Of course, that was before his sexy wife decided to start a dialogue—and while she was still wearing his old T-shirt and those satin boxer shorts.

"About last night—"

He didn't know where that introduction was going to lead, but the last thing he wanted was to talk about sex they weren't having.

"You were right to put on the brakes," he interjected. "I was out of line and I promise it won't happen again."

He figured that was what she wanted him to say, that she wanted him to take the responsibility and the blame. But she nibbled on her lower lip, seeming more confused than relieved by his assurance.

"You changed your mind…about wanting to have…sex?"

And how the hell was he supposed to respond to that?

He could say, "Yes, I changed my mind," except that was a blatant lie. Or he could say, "I'm a guy—we always want sex," and while that might be closer to the truth, he didn't imagine she would find it reassuring. He decided to aim for something closer to middle ground.

"I agree that intimacy between us could create more problems than it solves."

"So…you're okay with the 'no sex for a year' thing?"

"*Okay* might be a stretch," he admitted. "But I think I can manage to resist the temptation." Of course, it would be a lot easier to resist the temptation if she'd put some clothes on.

"Why do I feel both reassured and insulted?"

He managed a smile in response to her dry tone. "I'm just agreeing that sex would change things."

"I want to change things."

Though her gaze was steady, he heard the waver in her voice. He thought he understood now what she was trying to say, and he hated to think that he'd pressured her. "Kenna, I don't expect—"

The rest of the words stuck in his throat when she reached for the hem of her shirt and began to inch it upward.

His jaw fell open as the fabric rose to reveal a narrow swath of pale skin. The hem inched higher, that narrow swath grew wider, and his body was suddenly paying very close and careful attention. His avid gaze followed the rising shirt, to the bottom of her rib cage, to the gently curved undersides of her breasts.

"What—" He swallowed. "What are you doing?"

She tugged the garment over her head and tossed it aside. "I'm trying to tell you that I want to have sex."

"Kenna…"

She hooked her fingers into the waistband of those little shorts, slid them slowly over her hips, then let them fall to the floor. "Yes?"

His eyes raked over her, boldly, hungrily, from the tips of her crimson-painted toenails, up those endlessly long legs to the delicate triangle of pale curls at the apex of her thighs, over the slight flare of her hips, the indent of her waist, the long narrow torso, the luscious curve of her breasts—plump and round and centered with tight pink nipples.

He scrambled to hold on to some semblance of reason, not an easy task when all of the blood had drained out of his head and migrated south. And then he met her gaze, and it was her eyes—the fears and uncertainties swirling in the blue depths—that completely undid him.

What was she afraid of?

Did she really think that he would reject her?

That he *could?*

Kenna held her breath, silently praying that he would make the next move.

She'd laid herself bare—literally—and he was just standing there with a shell-shocked expression on his face.

Obviously she'd surprised him. She'd surprised herself, too. But once she set a course, she rarely deviated from it, and sex with Daniel was her ultimate destination.

But if it was going to happen, she really needed him to cooperate.

She didn't know the first thing about seducing a man. She'd read extensively on any number of subjects, including sex, but right now, she couldn't seem to recall any of the information she'd absorbed from documented studies or scientific research. What had inexplicably come to mind was a quote from an article in a magazine that she'd thumbed through in the staff room after confiscating it from one of her students. *Women worry about how they look naked—whether their hips are too wide or their breasts are too small. Men just care about the naked part.*

She had no idea if it was a universal truth or one man's personal opinion, but she was gratified to realize that "the naked part" seemed to have affected Daniel. His body's response to her awkward striptease wasn't hidden by the towel slung around his hips, and the obvious evidence of his arousal bolstered her confidence and calmed her nerves.

Then she looked into his eyes, and the blatant heat and intense longing in his gaze nearly made her knees buckle.

Everything Daniel did, he did with focus and intensity. She had no doubt that he would be an attentive and ardent lover, that she would enjoy an experience beyond anything she'd ever imagined. But what if she disappointed him?

Nerves and doubts swirled anew. Then he took a step forward and laid a hand on her cheek. Despite the gentleness of his touch, she felt the tension in him, desire tightly leashed.

"You need to be sure," he told her.

Though she wasn't nearly as confident as she wanted to be, she had no doubts about what she wanted. "I'm sure."

She curled her fingers around his wrist and guided his hand from her cheek…to her breast.

A muscle in his jaw jumped, but he held her gaze as his thumb brushed over her already peaked nipple. A fiery jolt speared from her breast to her belly, causing the breath to shudder out of her lungs.

The fire in his eyes blazed impossibly brighter, eliminating any doubts about his desire for her. He lifted his other hand to her other breast, brushed that thumb over that nipple, inciting another fiery jolt.

She wanted to savor every moment of this experience—to bask in the glory of making love with Daniel. She wanted to remember every touch, every taste, every insignificant little detail of the most significant experience in her life and seal them in her mind forever.

But when he touched her…she couldn't think. There was no time to absorb, no room for reason, there was only sensation upon sensation, exquisitely layered and infinitely complex.

She gave up trying to think or plan and let her instincts guide her. She wanted to touch him as he was touching her, to please him as he was pleasing her. She didn't let her inexperience hold her back, and she didn't let herself think about the women he'd been with before her, women with undoubtedly more practice and skill than she. Because she was the one who was here with him now; she was the one he wanted now. The realization was both liberating and empowering.

She slid her hands up his chest, desperate to feel his skin beneath her palms. And…mmm. Those muscles were as hard as they looked. She kissed his chest, breathed in the fresh-from-the-shower scent of him and felt her head spin with giddy excitement that this was really happening.

He shifted closer, so she could feel the press of his erection against her belly. She slid a hand between them, tugged at the towel slung around his hips and let it fall to the floor so that he was as naked as she. She reached for him, gasping with surprise—and maybe just a little bit of fear—at the size and strength of him. He caught her wrist when her hand dropped away and brought it back, wordlessly encouraging her exploration. She wrapped her fingers around him, tentatively gliding them up and down the smooth velvety skin, and was rewarded by a low moan that rumbled deep in his chest.

"You like that?"

"Yeah, I like that."

She stroked him again, and was rewarded with another rumbling moan.

"I like when you touch me—and I like touching you." His hands skimmed over her now, from her breasts to her hips and slowly back again. "You're perfect. Soft and warm and feminine."

She wasn't perfect. She wasn't even close. But the way he touched her, the gentle reverence of his hands and his lips as they caressed her, assured her that she was cherished, and that was enough. Then he lowered his head and swirled his tongue around the peak of one nipple—once, twice, before pulling it into his mouth and suckling deeply. And she knew that she was also desired every bit as much as she desired.

"And I love those sexy sounds you make when I touch you," he told her.

His hands moved from her breasts to her back, skimmed down her torso to her bottom. Then he cupped her buttocks and lifted her against him.

She was surprised by the move—and his strength—but instinctively wrapped her legs around his waist, gasping in shock and pleasure as this movement positioned him at the juncture of her thighs.

In two quick strides, he'd carried her to the bed and tumbled with her onto the mattress. And then he was kissing her. Deeply. Desperately. His tongue swept between her lips, stroked the inside of her mouth, made her shiver. His hands slid up her torso, tracing her curves, making her yearn. Every touch of his hands and brush of his lips made her ache and burn. She'd never felt so much, wanted so much. The onslaught of sensation was overwhelming, terrifying, exhilarating.

She felt a delicious tension building deep inside as he continued to kiss and touch, to taste and tease. She was pinned to the bed, and gloried in the weight of his naked body on hers. But she didn't just want him against her. She wanted him inside her, and she instinctively rocked her hips, creating a delicious friction as his hard length rubbed against her.

She was close to her release. Daniel could feel it in the tension in her body, hear it in her breathing. She was also pushing him dangerously close to his own.

He clamped his hands on her hips, holding her immobile while he desperately tried to catch his breath and not erupt like the teenager he'd been when he'd first fantasized about making love with her. A lot of years had passed since then, and he was determined to give her pleasure before he took his own. Her surprised responses and hesitant touches confirmed that she wasn't nearly as experienced as he, and he wanted to ensure that she enjoyed every single minute of their lovemaking.

"What—" She blinked, trying to focus eyes that were dark and dazed by desire. He had a pretty good idea how she was feeling. "Why?"

"Condom," he said.

"Oh." She blew out an unsteady breath. "Right."

"I'll be right back," he promised.

"Hurry."

He might have smiled at the urgency in her tone if he hadn't felt exactly the same way. It took him about three seconds to find what he needed in his toiletry bag, another four seconds to tear open the package and sheath himself. Those seven seconds seemed like an eternity.

Then he was kneeling on the mattress, parting her thighs. She opened willingly for him. His heart hammered against his ribs, banging a desperate rhythm that drowned out everything but his need for her. He braced his weight on his arms as he rose over her.

"I have to be inside you," he said. "Now."

"Yes," she panted her agreement. "Please."

Despite her obvious readiness, their joining wasn't easy. She was tight—a lot tighter than he'd expected. And he thought there was a moment, just an instant, of resistance. But he barely had a chance to wonder about it before she was lifting her legs to wrap them around him, pulling him deeper inside.

He started to move, slowly at first, desperately trying to regain the control that was sliding like a slippery thread out of his grasp. But it had been a really long time, and she was so incredibly and passionately responsive.

She let him set the pace but met him thrust for thrust, matching his rhythm as easily as if they'd done this a thousand times before. He'd never felt so perfectly matched with a partner, so completely connected. It might have worried him a little, if it hadn't felt so incredibly and undeniably right.

It was a long time later before he managed to lift himself off her. She murmured a half-hearted protest, then sighed contentedly when he wrapped his arm around her and tugged her close to his side.

His heart was still pounding and every muscle in his body was lax. No experience had ever left him feeling so completely drained, or so completely fulfilled.

He pried open an eyelid to peek at Kenna. Her pale, silky hair was spread out over the pillow, her eyes were closed and her lips were curved. The sheets had all been shoved down to the foot of the bed, leaving her completely and blissfully naked, and she didn't seem to care.

A quick glance at the clock confirmed that they still had another couple of hours before checkout, and as his mind considered various ways to fill that time, his body started to stir again.

He pulled up the sheet—not because he wanted to cover up her nakedness but because he didn't want her to get cold—and brushed a quick kiss on her lips. Then he eased out of bed to dispose of the used condom—and maybe retrieve another one.

When he walked into the bathroom and turned on the light, his head was still swimming with euphoria so that it took him a minute to put the pieces together. The tightness, the resistance, the blood on the condom.

He returned to the bedroom, no longer feeling relaxed or satisfied but absolutely furious.

"You were a virgin."

Chapter Nine

Kenna winced at the accusation in Daniel's tone.

She eased herself into a sitting position and pulled the sheet up over her breasts. Although his words had been more of a statement than a question, he seemed to be waiting for some kind of response, so she nodded.

"Goddammit." His eyes were blazing again, but this time with fury rather than passion. "How could you *not* tell me something like that?"

Her fingers tightened on the sheet. "Because I didn't want you to make a big deal out of it."

"Except that it *is* a pretty big frickin' deal." He stalked across the room, shaking his head. "You're twenty-six years old—how the hell is it possible that you've never..."

When his rant trailed off, she knew that he'd remembered. And when he looked at her, the righteous fury in his eyes had been supplanted by sympathy and apology.

She preferred the fury.

"Don't," she said, before he could say anything else.

"Don't what?"

She lifted her chin. "Don't you dare feel sorry for me because of what happened that day."

He went to his suitcase and yanked out his clothes. He seemed unconcerned about his nakedness, but despite the recent joining of their bodies, watching him dress seemed incredibly intimate to Kenna.

When his shirt was tucked in and his pants done up, he walked back toward the bed. "Are you saying that almost being raped when you were fifteen had nothing to do with the fact that you were still a virgin more than ten years later?"

"I'm saying that what happened back then had too much of an impact on my life for too long," she told him.

For a lot of years she'd been not just afraid of intimacy but ashamed of her body. The lingerie that she now favored was a deliberate choice that she'd made for herself, because it made her feel pretty and feminine, even if no one else ever saw it.

"Yes, almost being raped messed up something inside me," she continued, "so that whenever anyone got too close or tried to touch me intimately, I froze up. And yes, a lot of guys got frustrated because I couldn't respond appropriately to their kissing and groping. So forgive me for not wanting to ruin a moment of long-overdue physical pleasure by telling you that it was my first time."

He frowned. "What do you mean—you froze up?"

She dropped her gaze. She really didn't want to talk to him about this, but maybe she did owe him an explanation. "I mean that I'd suddenly feel cold all over, unable to respond, even if I wanted to."

"That didn't happen with me," he said, though she heard the note of doubt creep into his voice and knew he was worried she might have given some subtle signal that he'd failed to recognize.

"No," she confirmed. "It didn't happen with you."

But he still didn't look totally convinced.

"Maybe it was a trust thing," she admitted. "Maybe I didn't know any of those other guys well enough to let myself be intimate with them. Maybe it was easier for me to relax with you because I know you, and I know you would never hurt me."

He lowered himself onto the edge of the mattress. "I must have hurt you," he said, his tone apologetic. "I certainly wasn't gentle."

"You were exactly what I needed you to be," she told him.

"You should have told me. If I'd known—"

"If you'd known, you wouldn't have touched me."

"You're probably right," he admitted. "Are you sure you're…okay?"

"I have absolutely no regrets," she assured him.

"Really? Because I have enough for both of us."

"I'm sorry to hear that," she said, just a little stiffly. "I didn't realize my lack of experience would be so… off-putting."

"You have a way of twisting my words." He shook his head. "Your lack of experience wasn't a problem."

"Then what was the problem?"

"There wasn't a problem—except that your first time shouldn't have been with me."

"I shouldn't have given my virginity to a man I trust and care about?"

"You're doing it again," he grumbled.

"Doing what?"

"Twisting my words."

"Then tell me what you're trying to say."

"I'm trying to say…" He trailed off, as if not entirely certain how he wanted to finish the statement. "It shouldn't have happened, and it's not going to happen again."

She lifted her chin, ignored the tears that burned her eyes. "Well, I guess that's clear enough."

Daniel scrubbed his hands over his face.

He'd bribed his best friend to marry him, callously taken

her virginity, and now a few carelessly spoken words had pushed her to the verge of tears.

He should shut up. There was no way to make this better. There was nothing he could say or do that would change any of those facts.

Except that when he considered what she'd told him about her inability to respond to other men combined with his complete dismissal of what they'd shared together, he knew that she wasn't seeing anything clearly.

"Could you please put some clothes on so I can focus on this conversation instead of the fact that you're naked beneath that sheet?"

The blunt request had her eyes going wide and her cheeks filling with color, but she made no move to get out of the bed.

"Could you give me some privacy?" she finally asked.

"I've already seen and touched every inch of you," he couldn't resist pointing out.

"And made it known you weren't interested in doing so again," she reminded him.

"Another miscommunication."

Her brow furrowed at that.

He moved toward the door. "I'm going to get coffee from the café downstairs—you've got five minutes."

The elevator stopped on the fourth floor, where his cousin Justin and a woman got in. Justin nodded in greeting, though his focus remained on his female companion. Daniel recognized the woman as one of the bridesmaids. He thought her name was Tracey or Stacey or something similar, and that she was a cousin of the bride.

He couldn't help but notice that Tracey/Stacey had beard burn on her neck and Justin looked tired, as if he hadn't slept much the previous night, but the lazy smile that curved his lips in response to something the bridesmaid said suggested that he didn't mind.

Daniel tried not to resent his cousin's smug and casual

attitude. Obviously Justin had spent the night having great sex with a woman he wouldn't ever have to see again after today. Daniel, on the other hand, had experienced what was probably the most amazing sex of his life with the woman who happened to be his wife—there was no way for him to walk away from that.

He'd wanted her in his bed, but that was when he'd believed they were on the same playing field. The truth was, she didn't even know the rules of the game. Discovering that truth had been a shock; knowing that no other man had ever done the things he'd done with her had been an incredible turn-on.

Justin and Tracey/Stacey headed to the breakfast buffet in the restaurant, while Daniel went to the café to get the coffee he'd promised Kenna. Since the thought of breakfast had his stomach grumbling, he decided to get an egg-and-bacon sandwich on a croissant for himself and a cinnamon-raisin bagel with cream cheese for Kenna.

Although he would hardly consider himself an expert on human nature, he had enough experience with women to believe that they had fundamentally different attitudes than men about sex. Men could enjoy sex on a purely physical level; women tended to tangle it up with emotions.

Not all women and not all the time, but he'd seen it happen often enough to anticipate it when he took a woman to his bed. And the more frequently a man had sex with the same woman, the more likely she was to claim an emotional connection.

Because of their friendship, he and Kenna already shared an emotional connection that would only deepen if they added physical intimacy to the equation. A deeper emotional connection might result in one or both of them falling in love, and since he'd want to tear apart any man who ever broke her heart, there was no way he could put himself in a position to do so.

Which led him to the regrettable but inevitable conclusion that sharing further intimacies with his wife would be a monumental mistake. Now he only had to find the right words to explain that to Kenna in a way that wouldn't result in her wanting to throw something at his head.

When he got back to their room, he was relieved to find that she was not only dressed but packed, her bag waiting at the door. She was seated at the bistro-style table by the window, thumbing through the real estate section of the hotel's complimentary newspaper. It didn't matter to her that the listings would all be for Massachusetts properties and she lived in North Carolina. She always liked to look at houses for sale, and he knew it was her dream to someday live in a house of her own.

She accepted the bagel and coffee he offered with a murmured "Thanks." He'd just set his breakfast sandwich on the table across from her when he felt the vibration of his phone.

He pulled it out of his pocket and glanced at the screen, his thumb hovering over the ignore button. Most likely it was Josh, and he could call him back after he'd smoothed things over with Kenna.

The display read Archer, Calvin.

He hadn't heard from the man since his trip to Kentucky, and he was eager to know why he was calling now. "I'm sorry—I have to take this," he said.

Kenna didn't even look at him. "Of course."

Reminding himself that he would have plenty of time to explain everything to her later, he connected the call.

"Hey, Daniel—it's Archie."

"How are you, Archie?"

"On my way to the airport," he said. "I've got a meeting in North Carolina this afternoon, and I was hoping we might be able to get together after that."

"That would be great," Daniel agreed. "But I'm out of town right now myself, just getting ready to head back. Did you have a specific time in mind?"

"What works for you?"

He mentally calculated, adding travel time from the airport back to Charisma to their scheduled arrival in Raleigh and including a bit of a buffer. "How does six o'clock sound?"

"Sounds like dinnertime to me. You got any good steak places in Charisma?"

"As a matter of fact, we do."

"You make the reservation for three—my treat."

"Three?"

"I want to meet your wife."

"Oh…um…" He glanced at Kenna, who was thumbing through the newspaper as she nibbled on her bagel and paying zero attention to his conversation. What would she say about Archie's invitation? Would she go along with the request? He was reluctant to ask anything of her right now, but he didn't see that he had any choice. "Okay."

"You're not worried I might talk her into running off with me, are you?" Archie joked.

"You're a smooth talker, but not that smooth," Daniel bantered back, though he was less confident of his wife's loyalty now than he'd been twelve hours earlier.

And wasn't that ironic? There was a time when he would have said that he knew Kenna better than he knew any other woman, until getting naked with her proved he didn't really know her at all.

As Kenna plugged her earbuds into the armrest and programmed a movie on the screen in front of her, she was glad that they'd flown from Raleigh to Massachusetts. Right now a two-hour-and-ten-minute flight beside Daniel on a plane was infinitely preferable to ten hours beside him in a car.

They never did end up having the conversation he said he wanted to have, and she was grateful about that, too. She didn't need to hear him say again that he was sorry for what had happened between them. And even knowing that he regretted making love—

No, she wasn't naive or idealistic enough to think that love had played any part in the joining of their bodies. It had been sex—pure and simple.

But even knowing that he regretted having sex with her, she couldn't. Because being with Daniel—touching him and being touched by him—had been the most incredible experience of her life. In the past, whenever she'd tried to get close to a man, she'd gone through the motions, pretending to enjoy herself and trying not to panic. There had been no fear or faking with Daniel. Being with him made her feel sexy and passionate and real. And regardless of how he felt or what he thought, she would always be grateful to him for that.

So why did she want to cry?

Why did she feel as if the same act that had healed her body had somehow broken her heart?

She fast-forwarded through the opening credits of the film, while he scrolled through data on his tablet. Probably research on potential sponsors for the car he wanted Ren D'Alesio to drive. After meeting Cal Archer in Las Vegas, he had hopes of signing Archer Glass as a primary, but so far, that hadn't happened.

She had to admit to a certain amount of curiosity about the man's call—and his request to have dinner with both of them. She'd been looking forward to going home—even if home was no longer her own apartment but Daniel's condo. She could escape to the privacy of her room there and finally shed the tears she refused to let him see. Except that now she was expected to put a smile on her face and play the happy wife for a potential investor.

On the plus side, Daniel had made reservations at the Rib Eye Grill, so at least she'd get a decent meal out of the evening.

As it turned out, Kenna got a lot more than that.

The window magnate had a quick mind, a booming laugh

and boatloads of charm, and she genuinely enjoyed meeting him. But much to her husband's dismay, the older man wanted to talk about any number of subjects that had absolutely no connection to Garrett/Slater Racing.

It wasn't until their dinner plates had been cleared away that Archie finally broached the topic, and then he directed his questions to Kenna rather than Daniel.

"So what do you think of your husband's plans for putting together a racing team?"

"It's something Daniel's wanted to do for a long time, and I'm proud that he's finally going after what he wants."

"Do you plan on joining him on the race circuit?"

"I hope to take in the occasional race." Although she and Daniel had never discussed the possibility, she suspected that admitting as much to this man would reveal more than she wanted to about her marriage. "But my job and other responsibilities usually keep me close to home."

"You won't be lured away by the prospect of drinking champagne in victory lane?" Archie asked, topping up her glass of wine.

"I'm not easily lured," Kenna replied.

"Careful," Daniel warned, covering her hand with his. "I think Archie's working up to asking you to run off with him."

"I might—" Archie winked at her "—if I thought there was any chance that your lovely wife might be enticed to say yes."

Kenna managed a smile, all too aware of the part she was expected to play. "I already said yes—to the man who's always owned my heart."

Archie picked up a fork to dig into the Mile High Apple Pie the waiter set in front of him. "You're a lucky man, Daniel."

"I know it," he said.

"I passed Garrett Furniture on my way into town," Archie commented, changing topic again. "Made me wonder why you're not putting that logo on your car."

"It might end up there yet, but that's not my call to make," Daniel explained. "I've always tried to do my own thing, independent of the family business."

"I've got one of those—a kid who didn't want anything to do with my business. She wanted to go to law school, and I respected that decision. Until she decided to become a bleeding-heart defense attorney." He shook his head. "So this network security thing—you obviously know what you're doing there. Are you going to give it up for stock car racing?"

"GSR will have one hundred percent of my attention and focus when it's required," Daniel assured him. "But for now, at least, I'm going to keep my day job."

"You should never give one hundred percent to business— any business," Archie warned. "Family and friends should be your priority."

Daniel nodded in acknowledgment of the advice, but Kenna noticed that his grip tightened on his cup.

She knew how his mind worked, and that he saw this conversation as some kind of test—to which he'd just given a wrong answer. And because she knew how important it was to him to establish a good rapport with this man, she attempted to steer the conversation back to a less contentious topic.

"How many kids do you have, Archie?"

"Four," he said proudly. "Two sons, two daughters and half a dozen grandkids between them."

"Are they all in Kentucky?"

"Only my youngest daughter and my eldest son and his family. The others are scattered around from Seattle to Sarasota." He finished his pie and pushed the plate aside.

The waiter immediately whisked the dish away. "Can I get you anything else?"

"Anyone want more coffee?" Archie asked. "Maybe a brandy?"

Both Daniel and Kenna politely declined.

The older man glanced at his watch. "My goodness—I had no idea it was getting to be so late."

"Just the check, then, sir?"

"Yes, please."

"Are you staying in Charisma tonight?" Daniel asked.

Archie shook his head. "I like to sleep in my own bed."

"What time's your flight?"

"Whenever I get there," he said, and grinned. "One of the perks of being rich is not having to rely on the arbitrary schedules of commercial airlines."

He offered his hand to Daniel, and shook it with enthusiasm. "Thanks for meeting me tonight—and allowing me the pleasure of your lovely wife's company."

"It was our pleasure," Daniel assured him.

"And thank you for the fabulous meal," Kenna added, offering her hand.

Archie took it, then leaned forward and kissed each of her cheeks in turn.

They walked out together, and when they'd exited the restaurant, Archie turned to Daniel again. "You're probably disappointed we didn't talk about the sponsorship you proposed in Vegas."

"A little," Daniel admitted. "But I hope we'll have that opportunity at another time."

The older man chuckled. "One of the things I've learned through the years is that you don't have to like the people you do business with, but business is much more enjoyable if you do.

"And I'll tell you something else," he continued. "Before I made this trip, I'd already decided that I want to see the Archer Glass logo on the hood of your car when the season starts."

"You do?"

Archie nodded. "But after spending time with the two of you tonight, I'm happy to know that I'll enjoy doing business with you."

"I'm happy to say the same."

A town car pulled up at the curb, and the driver got out to open the door. "Have your legal team send the paperwork to my office as soon as possible. Once the details have been finalized, we can send out a joint press release and start generating some buzz."

"I'll get right on that," Daniel promised.

With a final wave, Archie slid into the backseat of the car.

They watched as the driver returned to his position behind the wheel and the car pulled away.

Kenna looked up at Daniel and couldn't suppress a smile. "You look like a kid who just got a shiny red bicycle for Christmas."

He grinned. "A car is *so* much better than a bike."

"Not to a six-year-old."

He laughed. "This is… I can't even describe it. Do you know how huge this is?"

"I think I have an idea."

"We've got a sponsor." He swept her into his arms and turned in a circle. "A *primary* sponsor."

She laughed as the world spun around her.

And then she stopped laughing.

Her feet were back on the ground but Daniel's arms were still around her, and she was suddenly intensely aware of the fact that her body was plastered against his.

There was a sense of familiarity to being in his embrace, but there was also something different. This time, her body recognized and responded to his on a much more intimate level. Her nipples pebbled, her belly quivered and her body wasn't the only one that reacted to the close proximity.

He dropped his arms abruptly and stepped back. She looked at him, and felt as if her heart was breaking again.

"We had sex, Daniel. Considering your vast experience with the act, I didn't expect it would be such a game changer."

"And I didn't expect to discover that my wife was a virgin."

"So we're back to that again?"

"I was your first—you can't tell me that's not a big deal for a woman."

"I promise—I'm not going to imagine myself in love with you just because we had sex."

He frowned at that. "You can't deny it changes things."

"You didn't seem overly concerned about those changes when we were naked together."

"Because I'm a man and I'm weak, and you...you are amazing. Beautiful and warm and passionate."

She stared at him, trying to reconcile the words with his actions. "If you really think so, why don't you want me?"

He reached up and gently brushed a strand of hair off her cheek. "You've got it wrong," he told her. "What I really want is to take you home and make love to you again—gently, patiently, endlessly."

"Oh." She was suddenly breathless. "So...why aren't we doing that?"

His smile was wry. "Because that would completely annihilate the lines."

"Having sex once is okay, but twice is a bad idea?"

"Twice leads to three times then four, and suddenly we've changed the nature of our relationship. You're my best friend in the world, Kenna, and I don't want to jeopardize that for anything."

Since it was the same argument she'd made when he'd suggested that they get married, she could hardly fault him for feeling the same way. So she nodded. "Okay—we'll stick to being friends."

But he still looked worried. "What you said to Archie, about being with the man who owned your heart—"

"Just playing the part of the besotted bride," she assured him.

He nodded, accepting—and visibly relieved by—her explanation.

Kenna only wished she believed it was true.

Chapter Ten

When they got back to the condo, Daniel called Josh to update him on the sponsorship situation, then he drafted an email to his legal team—aka his cousin Jackson—asking him to forward the sponsorship agreement to Cal Archer. By the time he'd completed those two tasks, it was almost midnight.

To say that it had been an eventful day would be a massive understatement. From the time that he'd awakened, sixteen hours earlier, the day had been filled with emotional peaks and valleys. Making love with Kenna, fighting with Kenna, the silent plane ride with Kenna, dinner with Archie and Kenna, and finally restoring the status quo with Kenna.

Or at least pretending that they'd restored the status quo.

He'd meant what he said to her—she was his best friend in the world, and he never wanted that to change. But if he thought that going back to being just friends would be easy, he was lying to himself.

He didn't hear Kenna moving around and figured she'd already gone to bed. He was exhausted, too, but he headed to the dining room, where he kept a bottle of his favorite whiskey in the sideboard. Maybe a drink would help him relax and fall asleep quickly so he could stop thinking about how much he wanted to make love with his wife again.

As he passed the living room, he realized the TV was on. He went to turn it off and discovered Kenna there, asleep on the sofa.

Should he wake her up so that she could go to bed? Or should he pick her up and carry her to her room?

He immediately nixed the latter idea.

While his intentions might be pure, he wasn't sure he trusted himself to lay her down on her mattress and walk away. The prospect of waking her up was equally problematic, as it brought to mind the memory of how she'd looked when she'd woken up in his arms earlier that morning—the sexily tousled hair and heavy-lidded eyes, the softness of her body pressed against him.

He pulled a blanket off the back of a chair and gently draped it over her sleeping form. That was better. Now he couldn't see the rise and fall of her breasts beneath the pale blue sweater, or the sweet curve of her derriere in the slim-fitting navy pants.

He resumed his path to the dining room and poured himself the promised drink. As he lifted the glass to his lips, he heard Kenna mumble in her sleep. The words were indecipherable, but something in her tone drew him back to her. "Kenna?"

Her head thrashed from side to side on the pillow and she mumbled again, a plea or maybe a protest.

"Kenna." He repeated her name, louder this time, hoping his voice would penetrate the dream that held her in its grip. "I'm here, Kenna. It's me, Daniel. Wake up, honey."

He continued talking, his voice low and soothing, until her eyelids flickered and, finally, opened. It took another minute for the confusion to clear, and slowly the color crept back into her cheeks.

"Okay?" he asked.

She nodded and shifted so that she was sitting up, her back braced against the arm of the sofa. "I guess I fell asleep."

"I guess you did."

He offered her the glass of whiskey. Her hands weren't entirely steady as she lifted it to her lips to take one tiny sip, then another.

"Do you have nightmares very often?" he asked her.

She shook her head, her gaze fixed on the glass. "Never."

He settled beside her on the sofa. "Obviously 'never' isn't really accurate."

"Almost never," she amended. "It's been years…a lot of years."

Which didn't precisely narrow it down but substantiated his belief that the nightmares stemmed back to when she was attacked by her friend's brother. Daniel tried not to think about that day, because if he did, he had to battle against a fresh surge of fury and frustration. Rational or not, he blamed himself for what had happened. He should have insisted on driving her home; he should have gone searching for her five minutes earlier; he should never have made that stupid bet.

Over the years, he'd managed to push the nasty events to the back of his mind. And he thought Kenna had, too. But the fact that she'd had a nightmare tonight made him wonder if—

"Stop it." Her firm admonishment severed the thought.

"Stop what?"

"Thinking that my dream is somehow linked to the fact that we had sex."

It was downright scary sometimes, the way she seemed to read his mind. "You're saying it's not?"

"I know it's not."

"Then why tonight?" he challenged.

"Maybe because we were talking about it earlier," she

admitted. "But I promise, what happened between us did not bring back memories of Blake in any way, shape or form."

He believed her, but that didn't stop him from wishing that he'd been able to do more, so that the nightmares had never started. "You don't know how many times I've wished I'd been there sooner—"

"You were there when I needed you."

He slid an arm across her shoulders and pulled her close to his side. "I still want to go back in time and punch him again."

"And break your hand again?"

He flexed his fingers. "Yeah, I'd do that again, too."

Kenna knew she would have to face Daniel again—there was no way to avoid it. When she walked into her third-period chemistry class on Monday, she decided she would play it cool and act as if nothing had happened. Some of his friends—probably the ones who were in on the bet—knew they'd gone for pizza, but she didn't think any of them knew what had happened afterward, and she preferred to keep it that way.

She rarely wore makeup, but she'd borrowed from her mother's assortment of cosmetics to try to hide the dark circles beneath her eyes. She didn't want Daniel to guess that she'd had nightmares every night since Blake's attack.

The minute she spotted her lab partner, with his hand splinted and wrapped, she knew there was no way to pretend nothing had happened. She'd seen him flexing his hand after punching Blake, but she hadn't thought anything of it. And when he'd taken her home, he'd tended to her injuries without any mention of his own. Now her cheeks flushed with humiliation at the possibility that everyone would find out what had happened.

"Hey, Kenna—"

She flinched when Josh Slater, one of Daniel's best friends and a teammate on the varsity football squad, called out to her.

"—you're going to have to do all the writing today. Apparently our star quarterback got taken down playing football with his brothers and broke his hand."

She looked at Daniel. He shrugged, wordlessly confirming his intention to stick with that story.

"Your coach must be furious," she said, when she eased onto the stool beside him.

"He's not happy," Daniel admitted.

She dropped her voice so that it was barely a whisper. *"I'm so sorry."*

"It wasn't your fault."

But she knew that it was. *"I guess I owe you."*

"Friends don't keep score, Kenna."

She opened her textbook. *"Are we friends now?"*

He leaned forward, deliberately nudging her with his shoulder. *"I'd say we are."*

She tipped her head to look up at him. *"Do friends say 'thanks'?"*

He smiled. *"Yeah, friends say 'thanks.'"*

"Then 'thanks.'"

"You're welcome."

Was it any wonder that she'd fallen just a little bit in love with him that day?

Not all the way, of course. Even at fifteen, she'd been well aware of the fact that Daniel Garrett was way out of her league. But the way he'd stepped up to protect both her honor and her reputation made her realize there was a lot more to him than she'd assumed.

She handed him back his drink.

"Are you going to be okay?" he asked.

"I'm fine," she assured him, and touched her lips to his cheek before rising from the sofa. "And I'm going to bed."

"Good night."

As she snuggled under her covers, she sent up a silent prayer of thanks that their relationship seemed to be back on track. As incredible as it had been to make love with Daniel, and as disappointed as she'd been by his determination to ensure it wouldn't happen again, she knew that lovers—and even husbands—were easy to find.

But a best friend who could always be counted on was both rare and priceless.

About a dozen of Laurel's friends showed up to celebrate her twenty-ninth birthday at O'Reilly's. After the presents had been opened and the cake eaten, Jordyn—Daniel's cousin and the pub manager—came over to their table and snagged Kenna by the arm.

"I need to steal my cousin's wife for a few minutes," she apologized.

"But we're going to do shots," Laurel protested.

"I'll bring her right back," Jordyn promised.

Because the room was dimly lit, Kenna didn't see Daniel until Jordyn steered her right to the table where he was seated with Josh and another man she didn't recognize.

The smile that curved her lips was as automatic as the quickening of her pulse, which she ignored. She was determined to accept the limitations he'd put on their relationship and be satisfied with the fact that they were still friends.

"What are you doing here?" she asked.

"We're celebrating," Josh answered before Daniel could, greeting her with a warm hug.

Daniel's friend and business partner was the only person who knew the truth about their marriage, so when Daniel snaked an arm around her waist to pull her away from his friend and brush a lingering kiss on her lips, she guessed it was for the benefit of the other man at their table. And even knowing it was only for show didn't stop her heart from pounding or her lips from tingling. "What are you celebrating?"

"The signing of Lorenzo D'Alesio as the driver for Garrett/Slater Racing's number seven-twenty-two car."

"I'm Lorenzo." The other man offered his hand. "But my friends call me Ren."

"Kenna Scott," she said automatically.

"Garrett," Daniel corrected.

"Sorry—I'm still getting used to the new name."

Ren looked at Daniel. "Your wife?"

He nodded.

"You're a lucky man," the driver said.

"I know it," Daniel assured him.

Jordyn returned to the table with a bottle of champagne in a bucket of ice and four glasses.

"We were waiting for you," Daniel said, as Josh lifted the bottle out of the ice. "Because none of this would have been possible without you."

"I'm happy for you—you've worked so hard for this, and now you're finally going to have everything you always wanted."

"Yes, I am," he agreed.

Josh popped the cork and poured the bubbly, then distributed the glasses around the table.

"To the success of Garrett/Slater Racing," he toasted.

They lifted their glasses and drank.

Daniel offered another toast. "To our new driver."

"To fast cars and—" Ren winked at Kenna "—beautiful women."

"Your turn," Daniel told her.

"To the fulfillment of dreams," she decided.

Josh emptied the bottle topping up their glasses, and Ren went to the bar for another.

Daniel's arm was still around her shoulders, his fingertips gently stroking her arm. There was nothing overtly sexual about the caress—in fact, he'd probably touched her the same way a thousand times before. But now that she'd experienced the pleasure of his hands touching every inch of her body, the slightest contact seemed to generate a sexual response in her.

Friends, she reminded herself firmly.

"I should get back to Laurel's party," she said, and started to ease away from him.

Except that the words were barely out of her mouth when she saw Laurel approaching, a glass of wine in hand.

"Everyone else left," she pouted.

"I was just on my way back," Kenna assured her.

Jordyn delivered the shots Laurel had asked for and sent Kenna a sympathetic look as she put them on the table.

Kenna wasn't a heavy drinker. Between the wine she'd had with dinner and the champagne, she was already feeling a little light-headed, so when her friend nudged one of the glasses toward her, she eyed it warily. Then she sniffed the contents and winced. "Peach schnapps?"

"I thought you liked peach schnapps."

"Only when I was too young to legally drink it."

Laurel sighed and pushed her own shot away, sipping her wine instead. "When you're twenty-two, it's fun to be crazy. When you're twenty-nine, it's just pathetic."

Kenna reached over to squeeze her friend's hand. "You need to stop obsessing about the number."

"I need to get laid," Laurel said bluntly.

Then she glanced up, her eyes lighting with surprise and interest, when Ren returned to the table.

"Who is *that?*" she whispered.

Kenna looked at Ren objectively. He was a good-looking man, about five-ten with a lean but muscular build, warm brown eyes, a strong jaw shadowed with stubble and a quick smile. But she suspected it was the way he carried himself, with cocky self-assurance, that drew attention to him.

Though she had some qualms, especially in light of Laurel's most recent comment, Kenna introduced her friend to the driver.

They started chatting and, within minutes, Laurel no longer seemed to care that she'd been abandoned at her own birthday party. In fact, Kenna was pretty sure that if she left right now, her friend wouldn't even notice.

Apparently Daniel suspected the same thing, because he asked her if she wanted a ride home. She'd cabbed it to the bar with Laurel, so she was going to need one, but she wanted to know her friend's plans first.

Her gaze shifted back to Laurel and Ren. She envied her friend's ease with men, her casually flirtatious manner, her bubbly self-confidence. She couldn't hear their conversation, but the heated glances that passed between them indicated definite and mutual interest.

"Sorry to interrupt," she said to them, "but Daniel's going to take me home, and I wondered if Laurel wanted a lift."

"Oh." Her friend looked into the bottom of her empty wineglass. "Yeah...I guess I'm done here."

The words were barely out of her mouth before Ren smoothly swapped it for a long-stemmed flute of champagne.

Laurel smiled at him. "I guess I'm staying a while longer."

"Do you have cab fare?"

Her friend nodded, her gaze still locked with Ren's. Kenna knew she wasn't needed, but she couldn't help worrying. Laurel, by her own admission, had lousy luck with men, she was undeniably under the influence of alcohol and freaked out about her birthday. To Kenna, that was a dangerous combination.

She grabbed her friend's arm. "Can I talk to you for a minute—please?"

Though Laurel obviously didn't want to leave the table, she let herself be dragged to the alcove by the restrooms.

Kenna wanted to find the right words to express her concerns, but Laurel spoke before she could.

"Please don't tell me not to do this."

Which was exactly what Kenna had intended to say, leaving her with nothing.

"I know I just met him," her friend continued. "But he's hot and sexy and it's my birthday and I want to have a good time."

The bold and unapologetic statement didn't completely alleviate Kenna's concerns, but it reassured her that Laurel was fully cognizant of what she was doing.

"Then I'll just tell you to be smart and safe. And—" she hugged her friend tight "—happy birthday."

As she left Laurel at the bar with Ren and walked out with her husband, Kenna realized that instead of worrying about her friend, she should aspire to be half as brave as Laurel and go after what she really wanted.

And maybe someday she would be.

"Fun, Food & Fireworks" was the Fourth of July theme in Charisma, and the holiday was always celebrated in a big way. The buildings in the downtown core were all decked out in red, white and blue bunting; red and white flowers spilled out of enormous planters wrapped with huge blue bows; and the Stars and Stripes flew proudly on every corner.

The first major event of the day was the Independence Parade, typically led by local businessmen in period dress to represent each of the Founding Fathers. Then came high school marching bands and majorettes, equestrian riders, tumbling troupes and city officials waving from antique cars. There were also dozens of floats—many of them homemade, as well as fire trucks, pipes and drums bands, church groups, Cub Scouts, local sports teams, motorcycle clubs and service veterans.

The parade started at the college, proceeded east on College Street, south down Queen, then west on Plymouth, crossing over Main to finish at Arbor Park, where there was face painting and balloon animals for the kids, food vendors for the hungry and market stalls for the shoppers.

The forecast was for sunny skies all day, but when Kenna

came out of her bedroom in a white halter-style sundress with a short skirt that swirled around her knees and thong-style sandals on her feet, Daniel found himself hoping for rain. A cold rain that would force her to put on a jacket to cover up some of the tantalizing skin that was on display— and stop him from sweating every time he looked at her.

Over the past few days, he'd spent an inordinate amount of time reminding himself to keep his hands off her. But not touching her had done nothing to lessen his desire for her. Even knowing all of the reasons that they needed to maintain the boundaries they'd reestablished couldn't stop him from wanting her.

They managed to squeeze through the crowd and secure a viewing spot in front of the Sweet Dream Inn near the end of the parade route. After the procession had passed, they followed everyone else to the park. Because it was inevitable that they would run into friends or family, they walked hand in hand, maintaining the illusion that they were happy newlyweds.

Not that he was unhappy. On the contrary, his marriage to Kenna had given him exactly what he wanted, at least with respect to his business venture. Garrett/Slater Racing was no longer a dream but a reality. His personal life was another matter entirely.

His friendship with Kenna seemed to be back on solid ground, and he was grateful for that. But living in close proximity with the woman who was his wife and having to pretend that he didn't want more from her than the friendship they'd always shared was a lot more difficult than he would have imagined.

As they meandered through the crowd, they stopped now and again to exchange a few words with people they knew. They crossed paths with Lisa Seabrook, a former runner-up for the Miss North Carolina title whom Daniel had dated a few years back—when she was still Lisa Jensen—and her husband, Warren; chatted with Jennifer James—better known as JJ, the event planner who had helped with his parents' fortieth anniversary in May; and briefly discussed vacation plans with Elaine Cole, the principal of South Ridge High School, who was enjoying her first full week of the summer holiday.

"There's Becca," Kenna said, spotting her sister in line with a group of friends waiting to get ice cream.

"She's maneuvering well on her crutches," Daniel noted.

"She's had a lot of practice," Kenna told him.

"When does she start physio?"

"Not until the cast is off—hopefully in another couple of weeks. Of course, Sue Ellen has already told her she better figure out the bus route because she's not giving up any shifts at the diner to chauffeur her around."

"Which means that you'll rearrange your schedule as much as possible to be the chauffeur."

"I don't mind," Kenna said. "I remember how much I hated taking the bus when I was a teenager."

"But you took three different buses every day to get to school," he remembered.

"Yeah," she said, and sighed.

"What did I say that put those shadows in your eyes?"

"It wasn't you. I was just thinking about the call I got from Dean MacLennan. Becca's midterm marks weren't high enough to get her in. Technically, her application should be rejected, but he said he'd take another look after her final exam results are in if she'll also write an essay outlining her reasons for wanting to attend Hillfield."

"So why do you sound worried?"

"Because I'm not sure she does want to attend Hillfield. She just filled out the application to get me off her back."

"You can't make her choices for her," he reminded her gently.

"I know. I also know that Hillfield would be really good for her, but I don't think she'll even consider it so long as

Todd's in the picture. Not that I was going to admit that to Dean MacLennan."

"I'm surprised the dean didn't try to bribe you," Daniel said. "Guaranteed acceptance for Becca if you'd be willing to teach at your alma mater."

Before she'd taken the job at South Ridge, he knew that she'd interviewed at Hillfield Academy and been offered a position. There was no doubt that the money and the working environment would both have been better than what she had at SRHS, but she'd chosen to go back to the south-side high school because she believed the students there needed her more.

"He did," she admitted to him now. "But, recent evidence to the contrary, I'm not easily bribed."

"You were easy," he teased. "Just not cheap."

"Imagine if North Carolina was a community property state," she bantered back.

He just grinned and swung a companionable arm across her shoulders. Her very warm shoulders. He lifted his hand and noticed her skin was showing definite signs of being in the sun.

"We should find some shade," he suggested. "Your skin's looking a little red."

"I brought the sunscreen so I could reapply, and I completely forgot." She dug into her purse for a travel-size bottle and handed it to him. "I can't reach my back—can you do it for me?"

She didn't wait for a reply but turned so that he was facing her back. Her slim, shapely back.

"Daniel?" she prompted.

He flipped open the cap and squirted lotion onto his hand.

It's Kenna, he reminded himself. *My best friend.*

The internal reprimand was supposed to refocus his thoughts, to remind him of the boundaries of their relationship. Unfortunately, his body chose to focus in another direction, and stirred in response to the reminder that she was also the woman who had been gloriously naked in bed with him not so long ago.

He laid his palm on her back, and she gasped in protest as the cool lotion contacted her heated skin.

"Sorry," he said.

He squirted some more lotion on his palm, but rubbed his hands together to warm it a little before he slicked it onto her skin. His hands moved over her, massaging it in. His thumbs followed the ridges of her spine, then his hands stroked outward, over her shoulders, down her arms.

"Oh, that feels good," she told him.

Yeah, it did. And he knew he could help both of them feel a lot better—

Nope—not going there.

He lifted his hands away. "That should help," he said, handing her back the lotion.

"Thanks." She dropped the bottle into her purse, then bent down to adjust her sandal. As she did, her bottom brushed against his already semi-hard and aching groin.

She quickly straightened up and turned to face him, a questioning look on her face.

He shrugged. "I'm human, and you're soft and warm and sexy."

"You give more mixed signals than a turn arrow pointing the wrong direction on a one-way street."

"I never said I didn't want you."

"You just don't want to want me," she remembered.

"I'm trying not to blur the lines of our relationship."

"What relationship would that be—our friendship or our marriage?"

"Both."

"Your call," she said. "But from where I'm standing, the lines are already blurred."

"Because we had sex?"

She nodded. "You can't undo that, no matter how much you might want to."

"I don't want to," he told her.

"So why are we both fighting against what we want?"

"Up until two weeks ago, you were a virgin," he reminded her. "And while I hope you enjoyed the experience, I have trouble believing that the one experience was so earth-shattering you can't wait to repeat it."

"That's my point," she told him. "I'm a twenty-six-year-old woman with exactly one sexual experience. I'd kind of like to expand on that."

He scowled. "What are you saying?"

"I didn't think I'd ever have a normal relationship with a man. Every time someone touched me, I thought about Blake's hands on me, because that was the only experience I had.

"Now that I've been with you, I know sex is about pleasure. And I was hoping that having more pleasurable sex would help me feel more comfortable about physical intimacy, so that the next time I'm with someone else, I'll be able to relax and enjoy it."

His brows drew together. "Let me get this straight—you want to have a lot of sex with me so that you'll feel comfortable having sex with other guys?"

"I'm not planning on having sex with anyone else while we're married," she said, as if that should appease him.

It didn't.

"I can't stand the idea of you being with anyone else," he admitted.

"Make up your mind," she suggested. "Now you don't like the idea of me having sex with anyone else, but a couple of weeks ago you weren't too pleased to find out that I hadn't had sex with anyone else."

"I was just surprised to learn that my wife was a virgin," he reminded her.

"You used to tease me all the time about getting naked, and now that I want to get naked, you're backing away."

As he'd said to her at the beginning of this insane conversation, he was only human.

"Not anymore," he promised, and pulled her into his arms.

Chapter Eleven

Finally, Kenna thought, as Daniel's mouth crushed down on hers.

But her eyes had barely started to close when a familiar voice called out, "There are the happy newlyweds."

Daniel lifted his head and looked into Kenna's eyes. "I'm going to kill him," he muttered.

The "him" in question was his cousin Ryan.

"I'll post your bail," she promised.

But lucky for Ryan, he wasn't alone. He'd brought his cousin Tristyn as part of his search party.

"Search party?" Daniel said.

"The moms said no one could eat until everyone was there, so we split up into search parties."

"For real?" Kenna asked.

Tristyn's dark green eyes sparkled as she nodded. "We headed north, Braden and Dana went south, Justin and Jordyn took east, and Lauryn and Rob west."

"You should text the others to let them know we found them," Ryan told his cousin.

"We weren't lost," Daniel pointed out.

"But you weren't at the picnic site, and the rest of us are hungry."

Daniel looked at Kenna, sincere regret in his eyes. "I guess we better go eat."

She took his hand. "If you play your cards right, maybe I'll go home with you later."

It was a tradition for all of the Garretts to gather in the park for a potluck meal—not just Daniel's parents and his brothers, but all of his aunts, uncles and cousins.

Kenna had always thought it was interesting that David Garrett had three brothers and that each of those brothers had three children. The oldest of his brothers was Edward, and Kenna had met him and his wife, Mary, only once, several years ago, when they came to Charisma for a visit before heading off to see the world. Unfortunately, they ran into a storm as they were sailing around Cape Horn and they both drowned, leaving behind their three sons—Matthew, Jackson and Lukas—in Pinehurst, New York.

The next-oldest brother was John, and he and his wife, Ellen, also had three sons: Braden, Justin and Ryan. Then there was David, who, with Jane, had Andrew, Nathan and Daniel. And finally Thomas and Susan, who had broken the pattern by having three daughters—Lauryn, Tristyn and Jordyn—instead of sons.

The search parties had all returned and the tables were all set when Kenna and Daniel arrived, along with Tristyn and Ryan. Andrew's daughter, Maura—her face painted to look like a butterfly, complete with antennae on the headband that held her wispy blond hair away from her face—came racing over to hug both Daniel and Kenna. "I'm so glad you were found."

Daniel just sighed.

The senior Garrett brothers—David, John and Thomas—

went to the barbecue area to get the hamburgers and sausages they'd preordered.

The Fireman's Picnic was another Fourth of July tradition. Members of the local ladder companies served up various barbecue items with all of the proceeds going to benefit the children's wing of Mercy Hospital. Some families brought their own portable grills to avoid the long lineups at the Fireman's Picnic, but the Garretts always supported the fundraiser.

While the dads were hunting for meat, as they liked to refer to their task, the moms—Jane, Ellen and Susan—set out the rest of the food.

There was a lot of food: tangy coleslaw, pasta salad, green salad, baked beans, spicy potato wedges, tater tots (because Maura had said "pretty please" and her soon-to-be mom couldn't say no even though there were other potatoes on the menu) and corn bread muffins. For dessert there was ripe juicy watermelon and vanilla cupcakes festively decorated with red and blue sprinkles.

Conversation flowed as freely as the nonalcoholic punch, and Kenna found herself enjoying the family dynamics as much as the meal. She was particularly fascinated by the men—their interactions with one another and the women. Until she met Daniel, she'd never had a steady male presence in her life. Sue Ellen had occasionally brought home her boyfriends, but none of them had hung around for very long.

In direct contrast to that, David and Jane Garrett had been married for forty years, had raised three children together and still held hands. Kenna knew they didn't agree on everything all the time, but at the end of the day, they supported one another and stood together—and that was the kind of marriage Kenna hoped to have with someone someday.

In the meantime, she loved being part of Daniel's family. His parents had always accepted her presence without question. That would change, she knew, when they ended their marriage and she was no longer just his friend but his ex-wife. Even if she and Daniel were able to maintain their friendship, as they'd vowed to do, she suspected that she would be persona non grata as far as the rest of his family was concerned. But she pushed that thought aside for now, refusing to let it put a damper on her day.

When everyone had eaten their fill, the leftover food was packed away and blankets were spread out on the ground for the fireworks display. Now that the sun had gone down, the air was quite a bit cooler and Kenna regretted not having the foresight to bring a sweater. Until Daniel wrapped his arms around her waist and pulled her back against his chest, sharing his body heat.

"I have a sweatshirt in the car," he told her. "Do you want me to go get it?"

"No, this is good," she said, because the feeling of being in his arms warmed her more effectively than anything else could. And the thought of what they would do when they got home later heated her all the way to her core.

"So I was wondering," he said, his voice pitched so that no one else could overhear what he was saying.

"About what?"

"What you have on beneath that skirt."

She turned her head to look at him. "Excuse me?"

"Since the morning that I inadvertently discovered your lingerie supply, I've spent a disproportionate amount of time thinking about your underwear," he admitted. "And even more so since I walked into the laundry room and found several interesting garments on display."

"Delicates are supposed to hang to dry," she told him, grateful for the falling darkness that disguised the rising color in her cheeks.

"I'm not complaining," he assured her. "I just wanted you to know, since we've agreed that we're no longer ignoring the attraction between us, how much I appreciate your choice of undergarments. Especially the pale pink panties with the little ruffle at the back."

He had to know that just talking about her underwear was turning her on, and she decided two could play that game. "You mean the ones I'm wearing tonight?" she asked sweetly.

"Are you?"

She tapped a finger to her lip, as if trying to remember. "Or did I put on the dark blue ones with the little strings that tie at the hips?"

He slid his hands down her thighs to the bottom of her dress. "Are you deliberately trying to torture me?"

"Are you feeling…tortured?"

"Among other things," he said, as his fingers toyed with the flirty hem of her skirt. "I think this is nearly as short as that little skirt you used to wear in high school."

"That little skirt was school uniform," she reminded him.

He nibbled on her earlobe. "I used to fantasize about sliding my hands underneath it."

"I'm sure you had your hands under plenty of skirts at Hillfield."

"But not yours," he said, his fingertips skimming upward again, beneath her skirt this time.

She sucked in a breath. "You seem to have found your way there now."

"I'm trying to make up for lost time."

The husky promise in his voice nearly undid her. "Do we have to stay for the fireworks?"

"If we leave now, everyone is going to know why," he warned, and the low timbre of his voice close to her ear made the muscles in her belly tighten with anticipation.

"I don't care."

"We rushed through a few things last time. My fault," he assured her, continuing with the featherlight touches. "I couldn't seem to think straight when you were naked. But this time, I'm going to take it slow. I'm going to run my hands and my lips over every inch of your body."

She had never been so incredibly turned on, and he was barely even touching her. She wanted to touch him, too. But from the position she was in, trapped between his legs, there was no way to get her hands on him.

She could feel his erection against her back, so she knew he was as aroused as she was. And as his hands slid up her torso, brushing the sides of her breasts, she shifted back. Just a little. Just so she was tucked more firmly against him, so that she could tease and torment him with subtle shifts and wiggles. The growl in her ear confirmed that her efforts were succeeding, and made her shiver with heady anticipation.

"Are you ready to go now?" she asked.

"More than ready," he admitted.

He stood up and helped her to her feet just as the first rocket was launched into the sky.

They rushed through their goodbyes to his family more easily than they might otherwise have done because the pyrotechnic display was beginning. As they made their way through the park, she vaguely registered the oohs and the aahs of the crowd in response to the rockets that whizzed and whistled and finally exploded with thunderous booms. Even the barrage of light and sound of the big finale only seemed a distant echo of the rockets of heat and pleasure bursting inside her.

They were in his car and driving away from the park before the last burst of color had completely faded from the sky.

He'd promised to take it slow this time. After the deliciously torturous foreplay in the park, he wasn't sure that was a promise he could keep.

He closed the door of the condo at his back and pulled her into his arms. As he lowered his head toward hers, she lifted herself onto her toes to meet him halfway. Their mouths brushed, clung. Her lips were as deliciously soft as he remembered, and sweetly yielding. As the kiss grew hotter and more intense, her lips parted willingly, her tongue meeting his.

He couldn't figure out her dress. The halter-style tie was easy enough, but he knew there had to be a zipper somewhere, too, and he couldn't find it. He was actually thinking that he might just tear the garment off her when she took his hand and guided it to the zipper hidden in the seam of the fabric at her side. His hands felt big and clumsy as he worked the tiny pull, then the material finally parted and the dress slid down her body to pool at her feet.

His gaze skimmed over her, slowly, hungrily. "You weren't lying about the pink ruffles," he noted, his voice husky with appreciation. "Although you didn't tell me that the panties were part of a matching set."

"I thought there should be some element of surprise."

"I'm surprised." He traced the lacy ruffle that dipped into a vee between her breasts, and slid his hands over the matching adornment across her bottom. "And grateful."

"I like sexy lingerie," she admitted.

"Something else we have in common." He reached behind her to unclasp her bra, then slowly drew it away from her body. "But I like you naked even better."

"I like you naked, too," she told him.

"Soon," he promised. "I told you I wanted to take things slow tonight."

"That was more than an hour ago. Don't you think that's slow enough?"

He responded by picking her up and carrying her to his bed.

And then he was kissing his way down her body, blazing a trail of heat down her throat, over her collarbone. He made his way to her breasts, lingered at her nipples. Kissing. Licking. Sucking. Until she was panting and writhing.

He lifted his head to give her one of those slow, sexy smiles that never failed to make her knees quiver.

"I love those little sounds you make in your throat," he told her. "But tonight, I want you to scream."

She swallowed. "I don't think I'm a screamer."

"Let's find out," he suggested, and dipped his head between her breasts again.

The sensation of his beard-roughened cheeks scraping against her soft skin was deliciously erotic. Then his tongue traced a path toward her belly button, and circled around it. She instinctively tensed as he continued lower, her breath catching in her throat. "What are you—"

He touched his fingers to her lips, silencing her words. "Trust me."

"I do," she told him.

She bit into her lip as his teeth scraped over her hip, nibbled on her thigh. She thought she knew where he was going, but she wasn't entirely sure how she felt about it. As it was outside her realm of experience, she couldn't deny a certain curiosity mixed with wariness.

She'd known what to expect with sex—at least with respect to the mechanics. But this seemed even more intimate somehow, and—

And then his mouth was on her, and her mind went totally and completely blank. She didn't know exactly what he was doing, but she could feel his lips and his tongue on her and—

Oh. My.

Oh. Wow.

Ohhh…

Had he not been so thoroughly engaged in what he was doing, Daniel might have smiled. Because it turned out that Kenna was a screamer after all.

He took her to the edge—and over. And while her body was still shuddering and the echo of his name still hung in the air, he quickly covered himself with a condom and buried himself in the wet heat between her thighs.

She cried out again, arching up to take him deeper inside. He fisted his hands in the sheet, desperately fighting for control as he felt her pulse around him. Her eyes were glazed, her breath coming in short, shallow gasps. He forced his own eyes to stay open, to watch her, reveling in her innate sensuality and unbridled passion.

When the first wave had passed, he started to move, thrusting into her, pushing both of them to the brink. He gripped her hips, holding on to her as the next orgasm shuddered through her, and finally lost himself in her pleasure.

He was collapsed facedown on the bed, too drained to move, too sated to want to. He was hovering on the periphery of sleep, considering a quick nap to recharge for the next round of lovemaking with his sexy wife.

He felt a subtle shift in the mattress as she slid toward the edge.

"Where are you going?"

She went completely still, like a teenager who'd stepped on the creaky stair while trying to sneak out at night.

"I, uh, thought you were asleep."

He propped himself up on an elbow to better see her face in the dim light of the moon through the window. "Which doesn't answer my question."

"I'm going to bed."

"You're already in bed," he reminded her.

"*My* bed," she clarified.

He caught her arm and tugged her down onto the mattress again. "Why would you want to go to your bed when this one's big enough for the both of us?"

"Our agreement was separate beds," she reminded him.

"I'd say that what just happened here proves our agreement has changed."

"I know you had some concerns that I might make too

much out of this, so I thought sleeping in my own bed would help maintain some of those boundaries you're so keen on."

"Right now, I'm keen on you staying right where you are," he told her.

"You no longer think I'm going to use sex to sink my claws into you?"

"Actually—" he reached up to rub his shoulder "—I think you already did."

Her cheeks flushed. "I didn't mean to."

"I'm not complaining." He brushed his lips over hers. "I love watching you lose control. You're so incredibly passionate and uninhibited."

"I've never been passionate before," she admitted. "Even when I tried to stop thinking and analyzing and let myself go, it didn't happen."

"It shouldn't take that much effort." His hands were on her breasts now, to please her and himself. He loved their shape, their size, their texture. "The pleasure should be so much that your brain just shuts off."

"It does…every time you touch me."

He smiled in response to the reluctant confession. "Then I'd say the problem wasn't you, but whoever you were with."

Her brow furrowed, as if she'd never considered the possibility before. "Harrison said I was frigid."

"Who the hell is Harrison?"

"The phys ed teacher I was dating a few months ago."

"He's obviously an idiot who doesn't have the first clue about women."

She didn't look convinced.

"Honey, who are you going to believe? Some guy who was pissed because he didn't get past first base with you, or the man who gave you three orgasms already tonight?"

"Well, when you put it that way…"

"And—" he slung a leg over hers, pinning her into place "—the night's still young."

As it turned out, he didn't need a nap to recharge him for the second round. He just needed Kenna.

Afterward, while their bodies were still joined, he asked, "Will you stay here with me?"

She sighed contentedly. "Since I'm already here and don't seem to have enough energy to move, I guess I will."

As she fell asleep in his arms, he wanted to feel satisfied that he'd got the answer he wanted. But there was a tiny piece deep in his heart that recognized he hadn't just been asking her about tonight.

And that question was still unanswered.

Kenna was already up and making breakfast when Daniel got out of bed the next morning.

She was wearing his old MIT shirt again with those silky red boxers that barely covered the curve of her butt, leaving the rest of her long, lean legs bare. Her hair was tousled, her face bare of makeup, and she was still, without a doubt, the most beautiful woman he'd ever known.

Her iPod was clipped on the waistband of her shorts and her hips were moving in tune to music only she could hear. He stood in the doorway, watching her until she turned— and screamed when she saw him.

Holding the spatula to her chest, she plucked the earbuds out. "I thought you were still sleeping."

"Yeah, I got that impression," he said, grinning as he poured himself a mug of coffee, then topped up her cup. "Did you sleep okay?"

"Very well, thanks."

He sipped his coffee, thinking that there was nothing better after a night of intense lovemaking than waking up to a gorgeous woman making breakfast. "So tell me," he said, "why a woman with a fascinating collection of sexy lingerie would sleep in an old T-shirt and boxer shorts?"

"Actually I slept in the nude last night," she reminded him.

"Which doesn't begin to explain why you're wearing *that* this morning."

"Nostalgia." She slid the omelet out of the pan and onto a plate, then carried it to the table. "You were going to get breakfast in bed, but since you're up, you can eat here."

"That's for me?"

She leaned over to brush a quick kiss to his lips. "In appreciation of the spectacular sex last night."

"Spectacular, huh?"

"Do you disagree?" She retrieved cutlery from the drawer, set it beside his plate.

"I don't disagree—I just think you could add a few superlatives."

"If I gave you too much praise, you wouldn't have anything to aspire to," she teased.

He caught the back of her shirt as she started to move away and tugged her onto his lap. Her brows lifted as his hands slid under her shirt to her breasts.

"What are you doing?"

"Aspiring," he told her.

Her quick giggle turned to a lengthy sigh as he continued to caress her bare skin.

"Daniel."

"Hmm?"

"Your eggs are going to get cold."

"I have a microwave." He tossed her shirt aside.

She gasped as her skin was exposed to the cool air, and again when his mouth captured one of her nipples.

"And you have…some client thing…this afternoon," she reminded him.

"A training seminar," he acknowledged.

"Right. A training seminar," she agreed, and tried to wiggle away from him.

"That's not until after lunch." He stood up, lifting her with him. "We have a few hours yet."

"You still haven't had your breakfast."

"I'd rather have you," he said, and took her back to his bed.

Chapter Twelve

When Daniel finally left for his meeting after lunch, he promised that he wouldn't be gone more than a couple of hours.

He also told Kenna that he'd text her when he was on his way back, because they were planning to grab a quick bite out and catch a movie. But when her cell phone chimed shortly after three o'clock, the message wasn't at all what she expected.

Can u come get me?

And then she saw that the text was from her sister.

When Becca got her phone, before she started high school, Kenna promised that if she ever needed anything, she only had to call and Kenna would be there.

So when she dialed back and Becca answered the phone, her only question was, "Where are you?"

"At Belleview—" She drew in a shuddery breath. "The parking lot near the soccer fields."

Though Becca was obviously trying to hide it, Kenna could tell that she was crying.

"I'm on my way," she said, grabbing her purse and car keys as she spoke. "But it's going to take me at least twenty minutes to get there."

"'Kay."

Kenna didn't know what had happened to upset her sister, but Becca's muffled sobs tore at her heart. Her hand was on the door when her phone chimed to indicate another message. Daniel.

On my way.

He'd happened to mention that his training seminar was in Eastwood, which was a lot closer to Belleview Park than she was. Not that the park was exactly on his way home, but he could be there in less than half the time it would take her to drive from his condo in Westdale.

She immediately called Becca back.

"Daniel can be there in ten minutes," she told her sister. "Is it okay if he comes to get you?"

"Sure," Becca agreed.

She disconnected that call, then dialed Daniel's number.

"Hey," he said. "I just texted you."

"I know, but I need to change our plans."

"What's up?"

It didn't take her long to summarize the situation since she didn't have many details, but she told him where to pick up Becca, and he promised to be there in less than ten minutes. She hung up the phone, grateful that he'd always been so solidly dependable.

While she was waiting for them, Kenna got out the necessary ingredients for hot chocolate—one of her sister's favorite comforts. She had a plate of cookies on the table and started pouring the drink into mugs when she heard Daniel's key in the door.

She gave Becca a quick hug and her sister's lower lip wobbled, a telltale sign that she was trying not to cry. Kenna released her and handed her a cup, then passed a second cup to Daniel.

"Thanks. But I thought you might want me to go, so you could have some time alone with your sister."

She shook her head. "Stay. Please."

She was worried that whatever was going on with Becca might be bigger than she could handle on her own. Thankfully Daniel had always been able to read her pretty well, and he recognized her concern.

They sat down at the table with Becca. The unhappy teen had taken a cookie from the plate, but instead of eating it, she'd broken it into pieces so there was just a pile of crumbs on her napkin.

"They're not homemade but they're pretty good cookies," Kenna told her. "If you wanted to actually eat one."

"Sorry." Becca brushed crumbs from her fingers.

"Do you want to talk about whatever happened?"

Her sister's eyes immediately filled with tears, but she valiantly held them in check. "I saw Todd—" she swallowed "—at the Hollow."

The Hollow was the informal designation of an area on the north side of Belleview Park. It was a fair distance from the main pathways and sheltered by surrounding trees, which had turned it into a popular hangout with South Ridge teens. Kenna had overheard some of the kids in class talking about a party there one weekend and that the ground had been littered with beer cans and condom wrappers the next day.

She wasn't pleased to know that her sister was hanging out there, but she held that thought for now.

"Did you have a fight?" she asked gently.

Becca shook her head. "We didn't even talk. It's hard to have a conversation with your boyfriend when he has his tongue down someone else's throat."

"Oh, Becca." She reached across the table to squeeze her sister's hand gently. "I'm so sorry."

"He called me this morning," Becca said, backtracking to explain. "And asked if I could meet him at the Hollow when he got off work at three o'clock. But Mom told me I wasn't going anywhere else this weekend because I missed curfew after the fireworks last night, so I told him I couldn't. He said okay, maybe we'll catch up later, and that was that."

She lifted her cup, sipped her hot chocolate.

"Then Mom's boss called," she continued. "It was supposed to be her day off, but someone called in sick and he needed her to cover from eleven until seven."

"And you figured you could meet Todd and be back home before Mom, and she'd never even know that you'd gone," Kenna guessed.

Her sister nodded. "But when I got there, he was with *her*. Heather Tisdale."

Heather had been a student in Kenna's sophomore science class the previous semester, so she knew she was a year older than Becca. She also knew that a lot of the boys referred to her as Titsdale, because of her attributes in that department.

"She's been after him for weeks, but Todd promised that he didn't like her." Becca swiped at the tears that spilled onto her cheeks. "It sure didn't look like he didn't like her today."

She sipped her hot chocolate. "I probably should have just gone home, but I don't want to see him. And if any of his friends tell him I was there…I just don't know what to say to him."

Kenna could think of a few choice words, but she kept them to herself. Instead she said, "Do you want to stay here tonight?"

Becca sniffed, her red-rimmed eyes shifting from her sister to her brother-in-law. "Can I?"

He responded to Becca without hesitation. "Of course."

"I don't have anything to sleep in," she said.

"Go wash your face and then I'll take you home to get whatever you need," Daniel suggested.

When her sister had gone to do so, Kenna turned to him. "I'm sorry—I should have asked you first."

"No, you shouldn't have," he denied. "She's your sister and this is your home, too. Besides, isn't this why we have the spare bed?"

Her cheeks flushed. "I never even thought… I could snuggle in with her tonight. She might not want to be alone."

"I'd rather have you snuggle in with me."

"I didn't want to presume," she admitted.

"Wasn't it only yesterday that we agreed to stop fighting what we both wanted?"

She nodded.

"Well, I want you in my bed."

"I want that, too," she admitted. "And I'm sorry for ruining our plans for tonight."

"They're not ruined," he said. "Just changed."

"I didn't have a dinner plan," Kenna reminded him. "So while you're running Becca home, I'll head over to the grocery store and pick up a few things."

"I have a better idea—on my way back, I'll pick up pizza."

"That works," she agreed.

Because of his longtime friendship with Kenna, Daniel had known her little sister for almost as long as he'd known her.

Becca had the same delicate features, slender build and fair hair as her sister, but Kenna's eyes were as blue as a clear summer sky and Becca's were more lavender. She'd been a beautiful child with a smile that could light up a room and who favored cherry Kool-Aid and grape popsicles, hated all green vegetables and liked mushrooms on her pizza.

The quiet teenager in his passenger seat bore almost no resemblance to the girl she'd once been. The ends of her blond hair were now dyed black and the remnants of thick, dark liner ringed her eyes. He knew what had happened to her: puberty. The little girl he remembered was now a young woman, and trying to grow up way too fast.

Becca was silent until he'd pulled out of the parking lot, then she looked at him warily and asked, "Are you going to yell at me now?"

"Why would I yell at you?" he asked.

"Because I did something stupid."

"If you already know that what you did was stupid, you don't need me to tell you."

She was quiet for another minute before she said, "I shouldn't have told him that I couldn't go. If he'd known I was going to be there, he wouldn't have hooked up with Heather."

"So your boyfriend hooking up with someone else is okay because you weren't supposed to be there?"

Her cheeks flushed. "I'm not saying that. I just know that if I hadn't insisted on waiting to…you know…he wouldn't have been with someone else."

His fingers tightened on the steering wheel. "I really hope the 'you know' doesn't mean 'have sex,'" he told her.

"Lots of girls my age are doing it."

This was so *not* a conversation he wanted to have with Kenna's little sister. But since no one else was around, he felt compelled to set her straight. "And you think because lots of girls are doing it, that makes it okay?"

She shrugged. "I think it's okay to want to be close with someone you love."

"Wow—that's a good one. Is that what he told you?"

Her silence was answer enough.

"Do you really believe he wouldn't have cheated if you'd been sleeping with him?"

"He wouldn't," she insisted. "He told me that he loved me."

"He loved the idea of getting into your pants," he said bluntly.

Her cheeks flushed. "That's crude."

"But true," he told her. "Guys like Todd will sleep with any girl who's willing."

"How do you know?"

"Because I was one of those guys in high school."

Her eyes narrowed. "Why are you telling me this?"

"Because I don't want you to get hurt—well, any more than you've already been hurt," he amended.

"But...I love him."

"Do you?" he asked gently. "Or do you love being with someone?"

She nibbled on her lower lip. "I thought I loved him, but he said that if I really did, I'd want to have sex with him."

"You're too young—"

"Why does everyone say that?" she interjected.

"Let me finish," he admonished.

"Sorry."

"You're too young *and* too smart to throw yourself at some guy like Todd Denney."

"Do you really think so?"

"I *know* so."

She sighed. "I wish you had a younger brother."

"If I did, I wouldn't let him near you."

"Why not?"

"Because he wouldn't be nearly good enough for you."

"So what makes you think you're good enough for my sister?" she challenged.

"I'm not," he admitted. "But I'm grateful that she married me anyway."

They ate pizza for dinner, then hung out in front of the television, watching part of the race at Daytona.

Becca wasn't a big racing fan, but she didn't seem to be paying much attention to the screen, anyway. In fact, every few minutes her phone made some kind of sound, indicating either a call or a text message. A few times, she teared up again, but Kenna was pleased to note that she never replied to any of Todd's messages. In fact, after about an hour, she finally turned off the phone altogether, and she and Kenna talked for a long time about everything except Todd.

There were a few times when she thought her sister was thinking about more than her breakup with Todd, but when Kenna questioned her, she just shook her head. After Becca had gone to bed, Kenna asked Daniel if he thought there was anything else going on with her sister, but he told her to stop worrying—and then he kissed her so that she couldn't think about anything else.

Becca went home on Sunday, and Kenna spent the afternoon making final preparations for her summer class that was starting the next morning, while Daniel studied up on some new antivirus program. Sunday night, they had dinner with Daniel's parents.

The next few weeks were busy for both of them. Kenna was teaching, taking an online course to upgrade her credentials and helping Becca with her admission essay for Hillfield Academy. Her final exam marks had shown significant improvement over her midterms, but Kenna knew she'd still have to write something spectacular to get admitted to the program.

Daniel was juggling a lot, too, between his clients at S3CUR3 N3TW0RKS and trying to find more associate sponsorships for GSR. His work as a computer security specialist had always required some travel, but the majority of that had been within the state. Networking on behalf of GSR required him to go wherever the money was. Over the past few weeks, he'd been to Kentucky, of course, as well as Florida, Virginia, Pennsylvania, Ohio and Michigan.

During the second week of August, he went to California for a cybersecurity conference. Although it was only a three-day conference, with the added travel at both ends of the trip, he would be gone for most of five days.

Kenna was keenly aware of the three thousand miles

between them and, even after the first day, she missed him more than she would have thought possible. Her courses—both the one she'd taught and the one she'd taken—had finished at the end of July, so she had a lot more time on her hands now. And a lot more time to miss him.

She knew she was getting in too deep, that despite her repeated protestations to the contrary, she was falling for him. And along with the falling came the foolish hope that their temporary arrangement might become something more.

It was a dangerous way of thinking, especially when Daniel had never given any indication that he wanted anything more than a temporary wife. Their agreement was for one year only, and Kenna promised herself she wouldn't ask for more. To do so would only be uncomfortable for both of them. Instead, she vowed to enjoy every minute of the time they had together, so that when they went their separate ways, she would at least have the memories.

She'd only ever wanted the simple things in life: a husband, a home, children.

Maybe it was because she'd grown up without a traditional family. Her mother had never married, and although there had been various men in and out of her life, none had stuck around long enough to assume a parental role with respect to her daughters. Maybe it was because they'd always lived in trailers or apartments that she longed for a real home. Not a mansion or an estate, just a simple house with a yard where her children could run and play. She wanted a sense of continuity and stability, but mostly she wanted someone to share her life—someone to love her enough to stand by her, through thick and thin, for better and for worse.

She hadn't entirely given up on her dreams of having those things someday, but the more time she spent in Daniel's bed, the more she realized that her plan to gain experience and move on had been a foolish one. Because after sharing her body with Daniel, she couldn't imagine sharing it with anyone else. As for falling in love with anyone else, she didn't even know if that was possible when Daniel would always occupy the biggest part of her heart.

But for now, she was just counting the days until he was home again.

When she went to bed Thursday night, she was glad to know that it would be her last night sleeping alone. His flight was due Friday afternoon, and she planned to make fried chicken and dumplings for dinner. It wasn't a fancy meal but it was one of his favorites.

She awakened early the next morning to the sound of his voice calling out to her.

"Kenna?"

She pushed herself up in bed and brushed her hair away from her face. "Daniel?"

He came to the doorway, breathed an audible sigh of relief. "What are you doing in here?"

She glanced at the clock on the bedside table. "It's not even six-thirty in the morning—I was sleeping."

He half smiled as he moved toward the bed. "Okay—why are you sleeping in the spare room?"

"Because your bed's too big and empty without you," she admitted.

"This one's too small and crowded with me," he grumbled, but he disposed of his clothes and crawled in beside her.

She lifted her arms to link them behind his neck, drawing his head down for a kiss. "I'm glad you're home."

"Me, too."

"I thought you weren't going to be back until later today."

"I took an earlier flight." He quickly stripped away her T-shirt and boxers. "I missed you."

It wasn't a declaration of undying love, but it was more than she'd dared let herself hope for, and her heart gave a little stutter.

Then he wrapped his arms around her and pulled her close. She snuggled against him, loving the feel of his skin against hers. Judging by the response of a certain part of his anatomy, he was loving it, too.

But for now, he seemed content just to hold her. And with her head on his chest, his heart beating steady and strong beneath her cheek, they drifted into sleep together.

He'd been gone only five days, but when he boarded the plane in California, to Daniel it felt like forever since he'd held Kenna in his arms.

They'd been married for ten weeks and they'd been lovers for about half of that, but he'd already grown accustomed to falling asleep beside her and waking with her. Every morning that he was gone, he'd woken up with his arms empty and ached for her.

Finally, when he began to stir late on the Friday morning after his red-eye from California, she was there. In his arms. And he sighed with pleasure to feel her naked skin against his.

She met his kiss eagerly, hungrily, suggesting that she'd missed him as much as he'd missed her. His hands stroked over her body, stirring her desire as well as his own. He parted her thighs and, moving between them, found she was more than ready for him.

He loved making love with her. He'd known her for years, but this intimacy was still new and surprising. Even more surprising was the intensity of the connection he felt when their bodies were joined together. It was different from anything he'd ever experienced. Deeper, stronger and infinitely more real.

And it didn't seem to matter how many times he had her. The wanting never seemed to go away. He didn't necessarily think that was a bad thing, but it wasn't something he was accustomed to, and he couldn't deny that the intensity of his need made him uneasy.

He'd never been with anyone like Kenna. He'd never known anyone like her, inside or out of the bedroom. And the fact that they were friends before they were lovers added layers of depth—and complication—to their relationship.

But that was something he'd worry about at another time. Because right now, he was exactly where he wanted to be.

The following Monday, Kenna went to South Ridge High School for an early staff meeting in preparation for the new academic year.

She'd told Daniel that she didn't expect the meeting would take more than a couple of hours, but she planned to spend some time in her classroom, checking her supplies and getting things organized for the first day. Since he'd managed to carve some time out of his schedule around noon, Daniel decided to pick up lunch and take it to her.

Any concern that he might be interrupting was alleviated by the smile that spread across her face when she saw him standing in the doorway of her classroom with a paper bag from Eli's Burgers & Fries in one hand and a beverage tray in the other.

"What brings you to this part of town?"

"I had to drop something off for a client not too far from here, so I thought I'd see if you could break for lunch."

"You have this obsession with feeding me, don't you?"

"I seem to have an obsession," he agreed, setting the bag and drinks on her desk as he leaned down to kiss her.

"Knock, knock," a voice said from the doorway.

Though Kenna immediately stiffened, Daniel only eased his lips from hers and turned his head slowly.

"That's hardly setting a good example of appropriate behavior for your students, is it, Ms. Scott?"

"It's Mrs. Garrett now," Kenna reminded him. "And classes don't start until next week, Harrison."

"I hope you're Mr. Garrett," the other man said to Daniel, "or the rumors will really start to fly."

He nodded and opened the bag of food to unpack it. "And I'll bet you're the gym teacher."

"Harrison Ridgeway—junior athletics instructor," came the pompous reply.

Daniel popped a fry in his mouth. "In other words—the little kids' gym teacher."

The other man's face turned red, prompting Kenna to interject. "Was there something you wanted, Harrison? Other than to lecture me with respect to classroom decorum?"

Harrison's attention shifted to her. "Laurel tried texting you to see if you wanted to go for lunch. You didn't reply, so I agreed to check your classroom to see if you were still here."

"My phone must be off," Kenna said. "But as you can see, I have plans for lunch."

"Sure." He nodded toward the take-out bag on her desk. "Better eat up before it gets…cold."

Daniel heard the soft intake of Kenna's breath and knew the other man's word choice had been deliberate, and deliberately hurtful.

"Let me walk you out, Harry."

"It's Harrison," he corrected through gritted teeth.

Daniel walked beside him down the hall, until they were out of hearing of Kenna's classroom. Then he grabbed the front of the man's shirt and slammed him against the bank of lockers.

"Take it easy, man."

"Don't call me 'man,'" Daniel said, his voice lethally calm. "And don't ever disrespect my wife again."

"I have absolutely no interest in your wife," Harrison assured him.

"Good to know. But if I hear so much as a whisper that hints at anything different, you won't be able to get a job teaching hopscotch to preschoolers."

"You think you can threaten me?"

"It's not a threat, Harry, it's a fact."

The other man straightened the front of his shirt. "I guess

another fact is that I didn't have enough zeros in my bank account to get into her pants."

Daniel knew he was being baited, but the knowledge didn't prevent his hands from curling into fists. And although he was really tempted to plant one of those fists into Harry's face, he knew Kenna wouldn't thank him for it.

"There isn't enough money in the world to compensate for some shortcomings," he said instead.

The other man didn't have a response to that, because he stalked toward the exit.

Daniel waited until he'd pushed through the front doors before he turned around—and found himself face-to-face with Kenna. "Hey."

"Hey," she replied, keeping her tone carefully neutral.

"How much of that did you overhear?"

He looked so guilty, like one of her freshman students caught with his hand in the specimen jar, she wanted to smile. But she didn't let her lips curve, because she didn't want him to think that she needed him to ride to her rescue—even though she appreciated the instinct.

"Enough to be surprised—and relieved—that you didn't hit him," she finally responded to his question.

"I was tempted." He slowly uncurled his fists. "Old habits."

"But what he said wasn't completely off target," she reminded him. "I did marry you for your money."

He flashed his trademark cocky grin. "Yeah, but you love me for my body."

This time, she did smile. "Absolutely."

She was still smiling when they went back to her classroom to have their lunch.

It was only after he'd gone that she finally acknowledged the truth she'd been denying for so long. She did love his body, and his heart and his soul. She loved his gentleness and generosity, his sweetness and sincerity, his passion and his compassion. In fact, she loved everything about him.

Because she'd done the one thing she promised herself she wouldn't do when she agreed to this marriage: she'd fallen in love with her husband.

Chapter Thirteen

It had always seemed to Kenna that summer passed much too quickly, but this year, it seemed to fly by even quicker than usual.

She realized that her perception might have less to do with the season than her awareness that every day that passed was one day closer to the end of her one-year agreement with Daniel.

Since he'd returned from his conference in California, he seemed to be sticking closer to home. Though he still had occasional trips out of town, he was rarely gone for more than one night and never more than two. Even so, she couldn't help but miss him when he was away, and she vowed to make the most of the time they had together. She wanted to cherish every minute of every hour of every day that she was with him.

Near the end of August, Becca had another follow-up appointment with Dr. Rakem. After the appointment, Kenna took her shopping to get her new uniform and the supplies that she'd need when she started at Hillfield the following week.

When they got back to Sue Ellen's apartment, she was just getting back from work. While Becca went to put her purchases away, Kenna gave her mother a quick update.

Sue Ellen seemed nervous, as if there was something she wanted to say—or maybe something she was waiting for her daughter to say. And when Kenna pinned Becca's new physio schedule up on the wall, she finally revealed what was on her mind.

"I haven't had a chance to talk to you since that little issue…with the rent," Sue Ellen said now. "But I wanted you to know that I will pay you back."

Kenna had no idea what she was talking about, and she had an uneasy feeling that she didn't want to know. Of course, that didn't stop her from asking, "What little issue with the rent?"

Her mother frowned. "I just assumed… When I saw Phillip after the weekend Becca was with you and he said the rent had been paid, I thought you'd taken care of it."

"It was Daniel," Becca admitted, coming into the kitchen. "He gave the money to Mr. Townsend the day he brought me home."

And he'd never mentioned a word about it to Kenna.

But that was a matter to be discussed with him later. Right now, she had more pressing concerns.

"Why didn't you pay your rent?" Kenna asked her mother, her tone carefully devoid of emotion.

"I was short, because I lent some money to Charles," Sue Ellen admitted.

"Charles? The new boyfriend?"

Her mother nodded. "He promised to take me to Atlantic City, but he said his car wouldn't make the trip unless he replaced the alternator, and he wasn't going to get paid until the end of the month, so I loaned him the money."

"And where is Charles now?" Kenna asked her.

Sue Ellen's eyes filled. "I don't know."

"You haven't seen him since you gave him the money, have you?"

She shook her head, tears tracking slowly down her cheeks.

Kenna sighed. "You've got to stop falling for every story you hear."

"I have a generous and trusting heart," Sue Ellen protested.

Kenna wondered which TV talk show had given her mother that particular catchphrase. "That's great, except when your landlord wants actual money."

"And now he's been paid."

"Because Daniel paid him."

"I don't know why you're making such a big deal out of this—it's not as if a few dollars means anything to a Garrett."

"It should mean something to you," Kenna said quietly. "Especially when it's the difference between keeping a roof over your head or sleeping in the back of a 2003 Chevy Cavalier."

"I made a mistake," Sue Ellen said. "I thought I was helping out a man who genuinely cared about me."

"Why don't you focus on helping the daughter who genuinely cares about and depends on you?" she suggested.

Then she kissed her mother's cheek and walked out the door.

Daniel had dinner in the oven when Kenna got home. Granted it was a tray of lasagna from Valentino's, but she had enough experience with his cooking attempts to be grateful he'd chosen takeout. And really, no one made lasagna like Valentino's. He'd also picked up a green salad and some crusty bread, and he had candles on the table and a bottle of wine breathing.

However, his plans for a romantic evening with his wife

seemed in imminent danger of derailment when she walked through the door and he saw her face.

He tipped her chin up, kissed her lightly. "Crappy day?"

"How could you tell?"

"You get a little ridge—" he touched the spot between her brows "—right here when you're worried about something."

"I don't know that I'm worried so much as baffled and frustrated," she admitted.

He poured her a glass of wine. "Becca?"

She shook her head. "Sue Ellen."

"Oh."

She lifted the glass to her lips, sipped. "That's all you're going to say?"

"What else is there to say?"

"You could tell me why you paid her rent," she suggested.

"It wasn't for her—it was for Becca. And...for you."

"For me?"

He shrugged. "I knew that if they got evicted, you'd worry about finding them another place, helping with first and last months' rent, maybe inviting them to move in here."

She smiled at that. "As if."

"Anyway, it wasn't a big deal."

"It was," she insisted. "Maybe not the amount, but the result."

"When I took Becca home the day she broke up with Todd, there was a 'final notice' on the door."

"Final notice," she echoed, shaking her head. "So it wasn't just one month that she didn't pay."

"It was three," he admitted. "And Becca started to cry—again—because she thought they would be evicted."

"If she'd told me, I would have taken care of it."

"Now you don't have to."

"They're my family—my responsibility."

He reached for her hand, linked their fingers together. "They're my family, too, now—remember?"

"For better or for worse," she agreed.

"Richer or poorer."

She managed a smile at that.

"You're not alone anymore, Kenna."

Maybe not, but she didn't want to get used to him being around, because then she might start expecting that he always would be. And while she hoped he would always be her friend, she didn't want to count on anything more. Because when their twelve-month marriage was over, they would each go back to their own lives.

"If Sue Ellen doesn't pay you back, I will," she promised.

"It wasn't really a loan so much as an investment," he told her.

"An investment in what?"

"Ensuring that your mother and your sister don't end up on the doorstep. If they moved in here, we wouldn't be able to have sex in the middle of the kitchen whenever we wanted."

"We've never had sex in the kitchen."

"A definite oversight," he said, and drew her into his arms.

She laughed. "You've got to be kidding."

He responded by unzipping her dress.

"Daniel," she protested, albeit weakly, as he peeled the garment off her body.

"Yes?" He'd kicked off his pants and was sheathing himself with a condom.

"We are not... Oh." Her eyes closed on a sigh of pure pleasure.

"We are not what?" he prompted.

She wrapped her legs around him. "We are definitely *not* letting my mother and my sister move in."

"Good answer," he said, and began to move inside her.

"I think I forgot to thank you," she said, a long while later as they enjoyed the last of the wine after dinner had been eaten and dishes cleared away.

"For what?"

"For turning my crappy day into something infinitely less crappy."

He smiled. "I'd say it was a mutual effort."

When she fell asleep in his arms later that night, Kenna realized that she'd completely lost track of the number of days they'd been married.

And maybe that was for the best, because every day that passed was one day closer to the end of their marriage, and she was no longer anxious for it to be over.

Daniel finished up a project he was working on and skipped out of the office early to meet Nate at the Bar Down Sports Bar.

It was a fairly regular meeting place for the brothers if they wanted to have a beer and catch a game, so he wasn't surprised by the invitation. However, he was surprised when Nate said they had business to discuss.

Daniel arrived first and took a seat in a booth. It was fairly early in the afternoon, so there was only one waitress working the floor with Chelsea, the bartender, helping out.

He'd dated Chelsea, briefly, a few years earlier. They'd had some good times together, but neither of them had wanted anything more and when they'd parted, it had been on good terms.

"Hey, handsome. I haven't seen you around here in a long time." She put a glass of his usual draft beer on the coaster in front of him. "But I guess you have good reason to stick close to home these days."

"Obviously you heard that Kenna and I got married."

She nodded. "Congratulations," she said sincerely. "It took the two of you longer than I expected to realize that you belong together, but I'm glad you finally did."

He'd heard similar comments from other people over the past couple of months, and he never quite knew what to say. Everyone seemed to agree that he and Kenna had been headed toward the altar for a long time, and it made him wonder what they'd say if he confessed that he and Kenna were faking their marriage.

Except that he wasn't so sure they were faking it anymore.

"You really weren't surprised to hear about our wedding?"

"It was obvious, even back in high school, that the two of you had a special connection," she told him. "The only surprising part was that you got hitched in Vegas—I can't imagine your mom was too happy about that."

"She wasn't," he admitted, as Nate came into the bar and slid into the booth across from him.

Chelsea gestured to Daniel's glass.

"Same?" she asked Nate.

"Please."

"You guys going to want food or just drinks?"

"Just drinks," Nate said.

She nodded. "I'll be right back."

When she'd gone, Nate reached into the inside pocket of his jacket and pulled out a letter-size envelope with the Garrett Furniture logo in the corner. He passed it across the table to Daniel.

"What's this?" he asked.

"Take a look."

Daniel opened the flap and pulled out a check from Garrett Furniture payable to Garrett/Slater Racing.

"That's enough for an associate sponsorship, isn't it?" Nate asked.

"Yes. It is." He didn't know what else to say. Kenna had suggested that he ask the company for a sponsorship, but he'd been reluctant to use his family connections for the benefit of GSR. And maybe a part of him had feared that, family connections notwithstanding, they would have turned down his request. That Nate had gone to the board of his own initiative—because he needed the approval of the board for any significant expense—proved that he had faith in what Daniel was doing. The realization left him stunned, humbled and moved.

Nate nodded his thanks to Chelsea for the beer she set in front of him. "Okay, that concludes our business portion of the meeting."

"I wish all my meetings were that quick—and lucrative," Daniel remarked.

"You mean like your marriage?"

While he'd hoped most people would accept that his friendship with Kenna had grown into something more, he knew it was likely his brothers would suspect the truth about their marriage. But until now, they'd kept their thoughts and opinions to themselves. Probably because it was really none of their business, which is what he said to Nate now.

"My marriage to Kenna is between her and me."

"Except that when you married her, you made her my sister-in-law," Nate pointed out.

"That doesn't mean you have to assume the role of protective big brother."

"Someone needs to look out for her. You used to be that someone—until you took her to Las Vegas and married her because what you wanted was suddenly more important than your best friend."

Daniel scowled, unwilling to admit that it might be true but unable to deny it.

"Kenna and I were both clear on our reasons for getting married."

"So what was the deal? How long do you intend to keep up the pretense? Three months? Six? How long do you think you can play at being husband and wife before one or both of you starts to think it's for real?"

"We've been doing just fine so far," Daniel said.

His brother narrowed his gaze. "You're sleeping with her, aren't you?"

"Butt out, Nate."

"You are." He shook his head in disgust. "Ten years of friendship in jeopardy because you couldn't resist screwing your wife."

"It's not like that."

"So how is it?"

He scowled into his empty glass. "I'm not having this conversation with you."

"She was more than halfway in love with you before you married her," Nate warned. "You don't think sharing your name, your home and your bed have tipped the scales further?"

"Kenna knows me too well to fall in love with me."

His brother lifted his beer. "Well, I hope when all is said and done, the sex was worth it."

"Dammit, Nate, you know she means a lot more to me than a warm body in my bed."

"Does she?"

"Of course she does."

"Then maybe I was wrong," his brother allowed. "Maybe she's not the only one who's more than halfway in love."

He scowled. "It's a long way from caring for somebody to falling in love."

"If you say so." Nate finished his beer and put some money on the table.

"I know so," he confirmed.

But he worried over the possibility for a long time after Nate had gone.

Yes, he had feelings for Kenna. He'd even acknowledge that they were strong feelings that had grown even stronger and deeper over the past few months. But as he'd told his brother, it was a big leap from that to wanting to spend the rest of his life with her.

Their agreement had been for twelve months, and that was a lot longer than any other relationship he'd had. So why was he suddenly thinking that it wasn't long enough to really give their marriage a chance?

Why was he even thinking about giving their marriage a chance? And a chance for what? To make it real, as Nate had suggested?

He shook his head, refusing to consider the possibility.

He wasn't looking for anything real. His marriage to Kenna was simply a means to an end for both of them, and at the end of the year, they would go back to their own lives.

Except that suddenly the life he had before Kenna no longer seemed so appealing. The idea of going to sleep alone and waking up without her wasn't at all alluring. The prospect of sitting down at the table for dinner with only an empty chair across from him was unpalatable.

He'd had other lovers, but he'd never found himself thinking about any of them the way he was preoccupied with thoughts of Kenna. He'd certainly never missed any of them when he had to be out of town for a day or two, but he missed Kenna every minute that he wasn't with her.

Was that love?

He didn't know—he'd never been in love before. But he'd never felt about anyone else the way he felt about Kenna.

Because of the example set by his parents, he believed in forever-after love. But he'd also had a front-row seat to the heartbreak Andrew had suffered when Nina died, and he'd vowed to protect himself against the risk of any similar pain. But somehow Kenna had sneaked past his defenses and firmly taken hold of his heart.

Which would have been great, except that it introduced a whole new set of questions: What if he screwed this up? What if he lost her? What if she didn't feel about him the same way he felt about her?

Daniel was late that night.

He called Kenna just before dinner to tell her that he was out with Josh and Ren. She ate the flank steak that she'd grilled with peppers and mushrooms (and she didn't even like mushrooms!) by herself, putting the leftovers in the fridge for another day.

She was asleep before he came home, and although she woke up in his arms when her alarm went off, he didn't show any interest in lingering in bed. He mumbled something about an early meeting and went directly to the shower.

She was at physio with Becca when she got the text message telling her that he was going to Atlanta with Josh. She didn't begrudge him going to the race, but she did wonder why he hadn't mentioned his plans earlier. It was as if he'd decided to go at the last minute, and she had an uneasy feeling that he was trying to put some distance between them.

He got back late on Sunday. She'd waited up for him, and they chatted briefly, but when she asked if he was coming to bed, he said he was too wound up to sleep. He made the same or similar excuses over the next few days—and there was always an early meeting or a late dinner. She tried to talk to him, but he kept insisting that he was just busy.

Kenna didn't know why Daniel's feelings for her had changed. She only knew that they had. Just the previous week, it was as if he couldn't wait to get home to see her. Now he was manufacturing excuses to stay at work late and taking frequent trips out of town that he didn't need to take.

She missed the intimacy they'd shared—not just the physical intimacy but their friendship and the emotional connection that had always been part of it.

Because they'd been friends for more than ten years, she knew his pattern. He'd had a lot of girlfriends, but he'd never stayed with any one for any length of time, so she shouldn't have been surprised that he'd apparently grown bored. But it frustrated her that he wouldn't just admit it to her.

If he didn't want to talk about their relationship and analyze his feelings, that was his prerogative as a man. But he barely talked to her at all anymore, and she knew she couldn't live like that for another eight months.

When he came home from an overnight trip near the end

of September, she decided that she wasn't going to let him dodge the issue any longer. She wasn't really feeling up to a confrontation. She hadn't been sleeping well for the past several nights, so she was tired and a little queasy, but she knew she couldn't put it off any longer.

"I made an appointment to see a lawyer," she told him. "It's time to stop pretending that this marriage is something it's not."

"Our agreement was for a year," he reminded her.

"Which was never anything more than an arbitrary time frame," she pointed out. "You have your money, so there's no need to continue this charade."

"I thought it stopped being a charade three months ago."

"Why? Because we were sleeping together?"

He didn't respond.

"And if that's your criteria," she continued, "then I guess the charade has resumed, because we haven't shared a bed in more than three weeks."

"I've been out of town more than I've been in it during the past three weeks," he pointed out.

"I know. And I finally got the hint."

"There was no hint, Kenna. I've been busy. That's it. End of story."

She shook her head, and the room suddenly tilted.

She grabbed the edge of the countertop and drew in a slow, deep breath.

"Kenna?" Daniel took a step closer, alarmed by the sudden pallor of her cheeks.

Her only response was to exhale, slowly and carefully. "Maybe we should table this discussion for another time."

"I know I've been doing more traveling than usual over the past few weeks," he admitted. "Maybe more than was really necessary. But our relationship seemed to go from zero to sixty faster than a Monte Carlo in time trials, and I needed some time and space to figure things out."

"Well, you had plenty of both," she said.

And he knew he still didn't have all the answers. But the irrefutable truth that he'd finally acknowledged was that he didn't want to let her go. Not at the end of the year and definitely not now.

Before he could say anything else, he noticed that her pale cheeks had taken on a decidedly greenish tinge. "Are you—"

"Excuse me," she said, and rushed down the hall toward the bathroom.

Of course he followed. And heard, through the bathroom door, the unmistakable sound of retching. Now he was really worried, because Kenna didn't get sick. Ever.

He went back to the kitchen and returned with a glass of water. He heard a flush and knocked on the door.

"Go away."

He ignored the instruction, opening the door to find her still on her knees in front of the toilet. He pressed the glass into her shaky hands.

"I told you to go away."

"When do I ever do what you tell me?"

She managed a weak smile. "Almost never."

"Are you okay?"

She drew in a deep breath. "I think so."

"Something you ate?"

"Maybe. Or maybe it's a touch of the flu that's been going around at school."

"The flu?" he echoed dubiously.

She nodded. "I had six students missing from my first-period class yesterday."

"You never get sick."

"Apparently I do." She lifted the glass to her lips to take another tentative sip of water.

"Do you have a fever? Chills? Body aches?"

"No," she admitted. "But I've felt exhausted and nauseated for a few days now."

Daniel felt his own stomach drop as he suddenly recalled

a recent conversation with Archie. The other man had been bursting at the seams with pride having just learned that he was going to be a grandfather for the seventh time. Though he admitted to feeling some sympathy for his daughter-in-law who was "sicker than a dog—sleeping all the time except when she was throwing up."

Exhausted and nauseated.

Kenna's words echoed in his mind.

"Are you—" he swallowed "—pregnant?"

Chapter Fourteen

Kenna sucked in a breath as her head shot up. "What?"

"When was your last period?"

She opened her mouth to respond, then closed it again.

"Kenna?" he prompted.

"I'm...not sure," she finally admitted. "A few weeks ago, I think."

"You think?"

"I don't remember the exact date, but I'm sure I had it," she said, though she sounded anything but certain.

"Are you?"

"I'm *not* pregnant."

"How do you know?" he challenged.

"Because we were careful."

But had they been careful enough?

He remembered "the talk" he'd been subjected to when he was a teenager, his father's emphasis on always using protection along with the warning that no protection was ever one hundred percent effective and a reminder to always think long and hard about the possible repercussions every time he was intimate with a woman. Over the years, the use of condoms had become such a deeply ingrained habit that he didn't need to think about it anymore.

But he'd been a little more relaxed about it with Kenna—because he knew her, she was his friend, his wife and a virgin until he'd taken her to his bed.

"The morning after I came back from the conference in Palo Alto," he suddenly remembered.

"What?"

"We were both more asleep than awake." And he hadn't been thinking about anything but how much he needed to be inside her. "We didn't use any protection that morning."

Though he wouldn't have thought it was possible, her already pale face got even whiter. "But that was only once."

"It only takes once," he said bluntly.

"I know," she acknowledged, rubbing the back of her hand against her forehead as she did when her head was throbbing. "But what are the odds that the one time we didn't use protection happened to coincide with my fertile period?"

"Any odds aren't good odds."

She looked away. "You're right—a baby right now would be a disaster."

But she didn't sound as if she really believed it.

He knew that she wanted to have children someday. When Maura was born, she'd gone with him to the hospital to see his new niece, and she'd got that misty-eyed look that a lot of women got when they looked at babies.

He didn't doubt that she would be a great mother when the time was right—but the time was definitely not right. And even if she was ready to be a mother, he wasn't ready to be a father. He'd only begun to acknowledge the depth of his feelings for Kenna, and the possibility of a baby was enough to make him break out in a cold sweat.

"Right now it would be," he agreed bluntly. "I've got a lot going on with GSR in the upcoming year, and that's

where my focus needs to be. The last thing I need is to add
a baby to the mix, especially when this marriage was only
supposed to be temporary."

She nodded, looking so miserable he wished he'd found
a way to temper his thoughts and regulate his emotions.
But his mind had been spinning since she'd dropped the
bombshell about the lawyer, so he hardly knew what he
was saying or doing.

Before he could say anything else, she bent over the toilet
again. But there was nothing left in her stomach to expel,
and eventually the heaving stopped.

He rinsed a cloth and gently wiped her brow. Maybe
he'd jumped the gun—maybe she was just ill. Either way,
it was obvious she was hurting, and he didn't like to see
her hurting.

"Do you want anything?"

"I just want to lie down for a little bit."

She went to the spare room and pulled back the covers
on the bed. There was a book on the dresser and an empty
coffee mug beside it. He didn't know when she'd moved
back into this room, but it was apparent that she had, and
he wasn't sure if he was relieved or disappointed.

She tugged the covers up to her chin.

"I'm going out for a while, but I won't be long."

"Okay."

"Can I get you anything before I go?" he asked her.

She shook her head, her eyes already drifting shut.

This marriage was only supposed to be temporary.

Daniel's words echoed in her mind, decimating her foolish hopes.

She'd known that from the outset, of course, but over the
past few months, she'd let herself forget. She'd let herself
get caught up in the fantasy of playing house with Daniel,
being his wife in every sense of the word. And while she

hadn't let herself get so far as to imagine they might have a child together, she wasn't at all distressed by the possibility.

Yes, she'd made an appointment to see a lawyer, because she knew they couldn't continue the way things were. But she didn't really want to end their marriage—she'd only wanted him to realize that he didn't want to end their marriage, either. But obviously that wasn't going to happen.

She slept for almost an hour, then woke up ravenous. Though her stomach was clamoring for sustenance, she was worried that anything she put into it might come back up again. She found a box of crackers in the cupboard and poured a glass of water, and she nibbled and sipped, testing her stomach.

Was she sick? Or was it really possible that she might be pregnant?

And if she was, what would that mean for their relationship?

She laid a hand on her belly, and let herself truly consider the possibility for the first time.

To have a baby with the man she loved would be her greatest dream come true. And she did love Daniel. Unfortunately, he hadn't given any indication that her feelings were reciprocated in the same way.

Maybe it was just the flu.

She didn't feel hot or cold or achy, which were all traditional symptoms of the flu. Her breasts were a little tender, though, as they often were just before she got her period. Maybe she would get it today—that would certainly put Daniel's pregnancy theory to rest.

She dug her pocket calendar out of her purse and flipped back through the pages to answer, for herself, his question about her last period. She always put an asterisk on the date that it started because her doctor asked whenever Kenna went in for a checkup.

She went back to June, though she clearly remembered it starting just a couple of days after they got back from

Las Vegas. Sure enough, there was a little asterisk marking June 10. The next asterisk was on July 13, then August 8 and… She moved the calendar closer, scrutinizing every one of the thirty squares in the month of September. There was no asterisk.

But September had been an incredibly busy month with back-to-school activities, staff meetings and social events. And on top of all that, she'd still been taking Becca for physio three times a week, and each session was noted on the calendar. It was possible there was just so much going on that she'd simply forgotten to mark the date of her period. Or maybe, because she'd been so busy, it had thrown off her system. She wasn't one of those women whose bodies kept a strict twenty-eight-day cycle. In fact, it wasn't uncommon for her to sometimes go six weeks between periods.

But from August 8 until October 2 was…almost eight weeks.

She heard Daniel's key in the lock and quickly stuffed her calendar back into her purse.

"I brought you some chicken noodle soup from the Corner Deli."

"Thanks."

"Feeling any better?"

"I think so."

He set up a tray for her and she ate a little bit of the soup, then pushed the bowl aside.

"I brought you something else, too."

He handed her a bag from the pharmacy.

Kenna guessed what it was before she peeked inside to confirm it: a pregnancy test.

"Don't you think you're being a little paranoid?"

"Maybe," he acknowledged. "But I'd rather know than wonder."

"You want me to take this now?"

"I would think you'd be as anxious as I am for the results."

She was anxious and eager and scared. But there was a part of her that just wanted to savor the possibility a little longer without dealing with the reality of yes or no.

She went into the bathroom and read the instructions. The leaflet described "this convenient two-pack" as being designed to give a woman fast and accurate results with a second test included so that she could retest and confirm the results.

Kenna didn't even want to take one test, because she still didn't know what result she hoped for—positive or negative. There was a part of her that was thrilled by the possibility that she might be expecting a child.

But if she was pregnant, she knew Daniel wouldn't agree to a divorce. He'd insist on staying married and being a father to their child because it was the right thing to do.

Except that it wouldn't be the right thing for him—not if it wasn't what he wanted. And he'd eventually resent both her and their baby for trapping him in a marriage that was never intended to be anything but temporary.

As she watched the seconds tick away, she found herself ignoring the yearning in her heart and praying for a negative result. Because as much as she wanted a baby—as much as she wanted Daniel's baby—she knew it wasn't what he wanted. And she didn't want him to stay with her for the wrong reasons.

She took a deep breath, turned over the stick and started to cry.

He couldn't tell anything from looking at her, and she didn't look at him. She just handed him the stick as she walked past him and back to the spare bedroom.

His fingers tightened around the plastic.

His heart was in his throat as he looked at the window—then settled back in his chest when the minus sign registered.

He followed her into the bedroom.

"You're not pregnant."

"That's what it says," she confirmed.

"Are you...disappointed?"

"No," she said, although the tears that shimmered in her eyes suggested otherwise. "Yes, I want to have a baby someday, but not with a man who doesn't want the same thing."

Now that the panic had subsided, he found himself wanting to console her. "I'm not saying that I'd never want a child—it's just that right now, the timing—"

"The timing was never going to be right for us," she reminded him. "Because our marriage always had an expiration date."

"Actually, that was something I wanted to talk to you about."

She nodded, as if she knew what he was going to say. "It doesn't make any sense to continue the charade for another eight months."

"That wasn't what I was thinking at all," he said. "Yes, the possibility of a baby freaked me out, but only because we've been married such a short time."

"I'm not following," she admitted.

"The timeline that I proposed for our marriage was arbitrary, and I want to stop counting the days and months and give our marriage a real chance."

"Now I'm really confused," she admitted. "We haven't shared a bed for the past three weeks—you've barely even kissed me. That doesn't seem like a recipe for happily-ever-after to me."

"I needed some time to figure things out."

"And you think you've got them figured out now?"

He nodded. "I want to be with you, Kenna. I look forward to seeing you at the end of every day, and when I'm away and don't see you, I miss you like crazy. I've been thinking about my future, and I can't imagine it without you in it."

"And when you think about that future, do you ever imagine that we might have a family of our own?"

"I'm not saying never," he told her. "I just think we've got a really great thing going right now. Why would we want to mess with that?"

"You really think a baby would mess with that?"

"A child changes the dynamics of a relationship. I just want to be with you for a while—I want some time to figure us out before we complicate the equation.

"I just want to be with you," he said again.

And then he kissed her.

It felt as if it had been months instead of weeks since he'd kissed her. And in his kiss she tasted sincerity and passion and something else that might have been the love he claimed to feel for her.

Maybe she was foolish or maybe she was just weak, but she couldn't help but respond to him. She'd missed this. She'd missed *him*. His lips were gentle, his hands patient, and when he started to peel her clothes away, she had no thoughts of resistance. After feeling so lost and alone for the past few weeks, she needed this connection with him.

He guided her to his bed. The pregnancy scare obviously still at the forefront of his mind, he quickly sheathed himself with a condom before he joined her on the mattress.

She reached for him, drawing him down to her. He parted her thighs and entered her in one deep thrust. Her body immediately and instinctively responded. Her arms and legs wrapped around him, holding him close, as they moved together in a familiar and seductive rhythm.

As her body arched and trembled, she clung to him, loving him with her whole heart even as it was breaking.

Because she knew this was goodbye.

On Monday, Daniel had to go to Wilmington to install a new data center for a client. He was out of town for a total of ten hours, but when he got home just after six o'clock, the condo seemed unusually quiet.

"Kenna?"

There was no response.

He told himself there was no cause for concern. It was likely she'd gone somewhere with her sister, or maybe she'd decided to grab a bite with Laurel. Certainly there was no reason for him to feel uneasy just because she wasn't waiting at the door when he walked in. But the uneasy feeling persisted.

He went to hang up his jacket and noticed that her shoes were gone. All of her shoes. She'd kept them neatly organized and stacked in two rows of boxes at the back of the closet, but they weren't there. In fact, all of her clothes were gone.

He pulled open the top drawer of his bureau.

Empty.

As was the one beneath it, and the one beneath that.

He crossed the hall to the spare bedroom to check the dresser there, but he didn't get that far. Her rings were on the bedside table that no longer had a bed beside it.

She'd left him.

He was poking at the dried-out chicken and rice that didn't look anything like the picture on the front of the microwavable box when the intercom buzzed.

A quick glance at the screen that showed video feed of the lobby revealed that it was his mother. He considered pretending that he wasn't home, but she would have driven past his designated parking spot to get to the visitor lot and would have seen his car there. He hit the button to release the security lock downstairs.

"I hope this isn't a bad time," she said when he opened the door.

"No, it's fine."

"I met a friend for coffee downtown and then stopped at Buy the Book to browse around and saw that one of Kenna's favorite authors had a new release out today."

He took the book she offered and set it on the counter. "Thanks—I'm sure she'll appreciate that."

"She's not here?" his mother guessed.

He shook his head but didn't offer up any more information.

"Since I'm here, I also thought I should remind you that it's Susan's birthday on Saturday. Tom's invited everyone for dinner, and I wanted to make sure you and Kenna were going to be there."

"You know I'm always up for a free meal," he said lightly. "But I'm not sure what Kenna's plans are."

His mother noted the half-eaten microwavable meal on the counter. "Did you two have a fight?"

"I didn't think so."

"The first year of marriage is always the hardest," she said gently. "Even for a couple who think they know everything about one another, like you and Kenna, there are a lot of adjustments to be made. So whatever happened, I'm sure the two of you will work through it."

"I wish I shared your faith."

She touched a hand to his arm. "Do you want to talk about it?"

"I wouldn't know where to start."

"Why not at the beginning?" she suggested.

Why not? he thought, since his wife's defection signaled the end of their marriage anyway.

"That would be when I asked Kenna to marry me so that I could access my trust fund."

He glanced at his mother, wary of her reaction.

She didn't seem shocked. She didn't even seem particularly surprised, more...disappointed, as if she'd suspected the truth but had hoped otherwise.

So he continued, "We never intended our marriage to last. But since we've been living together, our relationship has changed, and now...I can't imagine my life without her in it."

"So far I'm not seeing the problem."

"Apparently she doesn't feel the same way, because when I came home from work today, I realized that she'd moved out."

His mother frowned. "She didn't talk to you about this?"

He shook his head.

"I think you're going to need to fill in some more details for me."

"On Saturday, we were talking about the future. At least, I was trying to work up to it. But in the middle of our conversation, Kenna rushed to the bathroom to be sick.

"I immediately suspected that she might be pregnant, and…I panicked."

"Oh, Daniel. What did you do?"

"I just agreed that having a baby right now would be a disaster. I didn't say it—she did. But I agreed. I'm just not ready to be a parent."

She smiled a little. "No one ever is—even those who think they are."

"But it doesn't matter," he told her. "Because she took a pregnancy test and it was negative."

"And you were relieved."

He nodded. "And then, later, after I'd had some time to think about it, I realized the idea of having a baby with Kenna wasn't half as terrifying as the idea of spending the rest of my life without her."

"Have you told her that?"

"I was going to—when I got home today. But she was already gone."

"Where do you think she went?"

"Probably back to her apartment."

"She still has her apartment?"

"Our original plan was for a one-year marriage," he admitted.

She shook her head. "Okay, disregarding that for now,

if you think she's at her apartment, why are you here instead of there?"

"I'm not the one who walked out," he reminded her.

"So you'd rather sit here with only your stubborn pride for company rather than open your heart to the woman you love?"

"If she loved me, if she wanted to make our marriage work, she wouldn't have left."

"The only way to know what she's thinking or feeling is to talk to her," his mother said. "And it might help if you actually told her how you're feeling."

He scowled. "How do you know I haven't?"

"Because you're a guy and most guys—including your father—would rather have a tooth pulled without anesthetic than talk about their feelings," she said gently.

"He did a pretty good job at your anniversary party," he said in his father's defense.

"That was after forty years of marriage," his mother pointed out.

"So why do you expect *me* to be able to put it on the line?"

"Because if you don't, you won't have a first anniversary to celebrate, never mind a fortieth."

Daniel took some time to think about what his mother had said. Or maybe he was waiting to see if Kenna would take the first step. After all, she'd left him—moving out of his condo and his life without so much as a note.

By Wednesday, he couldn't stand the silence any longer. He decided to follow his mother's advice and tell Kenna the truth about his feelings and ask her to give their marriage another chance. He didn't know if he'd be able to convince her, but he had to try.

He used to stop by her apartment all the time without ever giving it a second thought. Today, after she'd buzzed him into the building and he was climbing the stairs to the third floor, he had a lot of second thoughts.

When she opened the door, she had half a red pepper in one hand and a cordless phone tucked between her ear and her shoulder, but she gestured for him to enter.

She finished her conversation and disconnected.

"I should have called first," he realized.

"No, it's fine," she said. "I'm just making pasta, if you haven't eaten."

"I haven't."

As he followed her into the kitchen, he realized that, for the first time ever, he felt like a guest in her home. He didn't like the feeling, or the distance between them.

"That was Becca on the phone," she told him. "And the third time I've talked to her today. They're starting *Macbeth* in her English class next week and she wants to read ahead but she's struggling with some of the language."

"Is she settling in okay at Hillfield?"

"I think so. It's an adjustment, but one that she wants to make."

"That's good news."

She nodded.

But he hadn't come over here to talk about her sister, and although he warned himself that he might not want to hear her answer to the question, he had to ask, "Why did you leave?"

She looked at him with sadness and regret. "Because I don't want the same things you want."

"You don't want to be with me?"

She turned her attention back to the sauce simmering on the stove, but not before he saw the tears that filled her eyes. "Following the race circuit around the country is your dream, not mine. I want roots, stability, a family."

"The two don't have to be mutually exclusive," he told her. "Please, Kenna, cancel your appointment with the lawyer."

She shook her head. "I met with him yesterday afternoon."

"That was fast."

"I don't know that it was particularly fast. I called for an appointment and that was the date and time I was given." She started slicing up a cucumber and gestured to the romaine that she'd already washed. "Do you want to tear up those leaves for the salad?"

No, he didn't want to make the salad. He didn't want to hang out in her kitchen as they'd done so many times in the past and pretend that everything was okay. Nothing was okay. He'd finally realized that he wanted to spend the rest of his life with her, and she'd decided that she wanted to end their marriage. That was as far from okay as he could imagine.

But, of course, he didn't say any of that. Instead, he washed his hands and began the task she'd assigned to him.

"I'm glad you came by," she said now. "I've been meaning to call, but I wasn't sure what to say."

"We used to be able to talk about anything."

She nodded. "And I hope that someday, maybe, we can get there again."

"Is that really what you want?" he asked incredulously. "To be friends again?"

She dumped the pasta into boiling water. "I don't want to lose you completely."

"You didn't lose me. You walked out."

Her phone rang, and she wiped her hands on a towel before picking up the handset.

"It's Becca again," she told him, and stepped out of the room to connect the call.

Finished with the lettuce, he decided to take over chopping the other vegetables for the salad while she was on the phone. But because his mind was still speculating about the lawyer's visit, he wasn't paying close attention to what he was doing. The knife slipped as he cut through a carrot, and nicked his finger. He didn't even feel it at first and didn't realize what he'd done until he saw the bead of blood.

Since Kenna was still on the phone, he went to the bathroom to find a Band-Aid. There weren't any in the medicine cabinet, so he checked the makeup bag that was open on the counter. As he rummaged through, he found a familiar plastic stick.

He barely had a chance to wonder why she'd kept a negative pregnancy test when he saw that, in the little window where he had very clearly seen a minus sign a few days before, there was a plus sign instead.

Chapter Fifteen

Kenna had finished her phone call and was stirring the pasta when he returned to the kitchen.

"What the hell is this?"

She glanced up. "What?"

He held up the pregnancy test.

Her face went pale. "Where did you get that?"

"It was in your makeup bag."

"Why were you looking in my makeup bag?"

He showed his bloody finger to her. "I was looking for a Band-Aid."

She reached into the cupboard above the sink and pulled out a first aid kit.

He didn't care about his finger—it was his heart that was really bleeding. "You lied to me, Kenna."

She lifted her chin. "I gave you the answer you wanted."

He threw the stick, bouncing it off the edge of the counter, making her jump. "I wanted the truth."

"You wanted out of our marriage—no messy ties or responsibilities."

"I *never* said anything about wanting out of our marriage. You're the one who went to see the lawyer."

"You didn't say the words," she acknowledged. "You just made sure you stayed on your side of the bed—but that was only when you bothered to come home."

He scrubbed his hands over his face. He'd tried to explain that to her already, and he'd come over here tonight to put his heart on the line and ask her for a second chance. But all of that had taken a backseat to this latest revelation. She'd taken a pregnancy test and shown him a negative result. To find out that she'd lied…he didn't—couldn't—understand.

"Were you ever going to tell me the truth?" he demanded.

"I could hardly keep my pregnancy a secret forever."

"*When* were you going to tell me?"

"After the divorce was final. At least, that was the plan before I found out that North Carolina requires spouses to live separate and apart for a year before they can get a divorce."

His eyes narrowed. "You were planning to go ahead with a divorce even though you're having my baby?"

"You don't want this baby—"

"I don't know what I want. I've barely had two minutes to get my head around the fact that you're pregnant."

"You don't want this baby," she said again, touching a hand to his arm. "And it's okay that you don't. I'm not asking you to change any of your plans, Daniel."

He picked up the stick from the floor and looked at the little plus sign again. "A baby changes everything."

"You want to do the right thing," she noted. "But staying together for the sake of a child isn't the right thing for any of us if it's not what you really want."

"I came over here tonight to ask you to give our marriage a second chance."

"A second chance isn't going to change the fact that we want different things. You said it yourself, Daniel, you've got a lot going on with GSR, and that needs to be your focus.

"I'm not going to settle for stolen moments of your time and reluctant scraps of affection. I deserve more than that, and our baby deserves more than that."

"Are you asking me to give up racing?"

"No," she said immediately, unequivocally. "I'm just asking you for the divorce you promised me when we got married."

Laurel stared at her, stunned. "You really asked him for a divorce?"

"It's the only way I'm going to be able to move on with my life," Kenna told her friend.

"But you love him," Laurel said, as if that was all that mattered.

"Weren't you paying any attention to what I told you? Our marriage was never real."

"I was paying attention—Las Vegas, six million dollars, fake pregnancy test, blah blah blah."

Kenna smiled. This was exactly why she'd invited her friend to come over tonight—because no one knew better than Laurel how to make her smile through her tears.

"Actually, I am curious about the fake pregnancy test," Laurel admitted. "How'd you do it?"

"I dipped the stick in the toilet bowl."

"Clever," her friend said. "But why did you do it?"

"Because I knew that if Daniel knew I was pregnant, he'd insist on staying with me."

"And staying married to the father of your child—the man you love—would be a bad thing?"

"My feelings aren't the issue."

"They are," her friend insisted. "You walked out on him because you were afraid he'd break your heart. Now it's scattered all over the floor in a thousand pieces anyway."

"Yeah, watch where you step, will you?"

Her friend smiled, then sighed. "You really made a mess of things, didn't you?"

"I have no regrets," Kenna promised her.

"And what about your baby?"

"I'm going to be the best mother I can be to my baby."

"You're going to be a fabulous mother," Laurel said confidently. "But your kid's going to need a father, too."

"I don't know about that—I never had a father and I think I turned out okay."

"No father and Sue Ellen for a mother, I'd say it's a miracle you survived. But that's not the point."

"I didn't realize you had one."

"You're a teacher. You know the statistics. A child in a single-parent home is far more likely to perform below his or her peers."

"And you know statistics can be used to prove almost anything," Kenna rebutted. "But that study, which I did read, focused on kids in low-income families who had no contact with the noncustodial parent."

"So you're planning to work out a schedule for shared custody?"

"No." She put a hand over her belly, instinctively, protectively. "I just meant that I won't interfere with my baby knowing his or her father."

"What if Daniel wants shared custody?" Laurel challenged.

"He won't."

"How do you know?"

"Because he doesn't want this baby at all."

"Maybe not now," Laurel acknowledged. "Because he wasn't prepared for this. But you're not due until May, so he's still got seven months to get used to the idea of being a father. Maybe, once he does, he'll embrace the idea."

Kenna scowled. "Why are you doing this?"

"Because I want to make sure you've considered all of

the repercussions before you walk too far down a path that you can't find your way back from."

Kenna stubbornly fisted her hands in her lap. "I'm doing what's best for all of us."

The following weekend was Columbus Day.

Kenna knew that Laurel was planning to spend the weekend on the Crystal Coast because her grandmother, who lived there, was on a seniors' tour of Europe and had asked Laurel to check on her house periodically. And because she didn't want to sit at home for three whole days, Kenna asked her friend if she could tag along.

Laurel accused her of wanting a place to hide out where Daniel couldn't find her, and maybe there was an element of truth to that. But since he'd found out about their baby, nine days earlier, she hadn't seen or heard a single word from him, so maybe she was really afraid that he wouldn't even try to track her down. At least if she was out of town, she wouldn't hear her phone not ring or her buzzer not sound.

Early Saturday morning, Laurel decided that she wanted buttermilk pancakes. Of course, the basic staples that they'd brought up for the weekend didn't include buttermilk, so she decided to make a quick trip to the grocery store. She rejected Kenna's offer to go with her, pointing out that it didn't take two people to pick up a carton of buttermilk, and encouraged her friend to hang out and relax.

So Kenna was hanging out, if not really relaxing, when she heard the screen door open not five minutes after her friend had left. She was about to ask what she'd forgotten when she looked up and saw it wasn't Laurel in the doorway—it was Daniel.

Her breath caught in her throat as her gaze swept over him.

The nine days since she'd last seen him felt like a lifetime. She couldn't remember when they'd been out of contact for so long. Certainly not in recent years, because even if a few days went by that she didn't see him, they'd communicated via email or text messages.

He looked like hell, as if he hadn't shaved in three days or slept in twice that number. And at the same time, he looked really good, because he was Daniel and she'd missed him unbearably.

She swallowed, urging her frantically beating heart to exercise caution.

"What are you doing here?"

"I brought the separation agreement your lawyer sent to me," he said, tossing the envelope onto the table beside her.

And with those words, the tentative hope that had started to bloom in her heart was ruthlessly crushed.

That was it, then—she'd got what she wanted. Or what she'd told him she wanted, anyway. "Thanks, but you didn't have to bring it out here. You could have—"

"I didn't sign it," he told her.

"It's a standard agreement, so there shouldn't be any issues." Her lawyer hadn't approved of Kenna's complete relinquishment of any claim for property settlement or financial support, but she didn't know about the original agreement between the spouses. Kenna had already been paid one hundred thousand dollars for one year of marriage and, since they hadn't made it through half of that, she almost felt as if she owed Daniel money.

"Except the standard clauses don't apply, because I do still want to live with you as husband and wife." He met her gaze, held it. "And I want us to raise our baby together."

He didn't say "the baby" but "our baby"—was it a deliberate or subconscious word choice? A reflection of his intention to take responsibility? Or possibly an indication that he felt connected to the child in her womb?

"I know we got married for the wrong reasons," he admitted, "but everything changed after that."

"Because we had sex?" she asked skeptically.

"Because I fell in love with you."

Even as her brain struggled to make sense of the words, her heart started to swell inside her chest. "You...what?"

"That was my initial reaction, too," he admitted. "And that's probably why I pulled away from you, trying to deny my feelings. But it's true—I love you, Kenna."

She shook her head. "Please don't do this."

"Don't do what?"

"Don't tell me what you think I want to hear."

"Since when have I ever done that?" he challenged.

"I don't know," she admitted. "But I know you believe in doing the right thing, and obviously you've made up your mind that being a father to our baby is the right thing."

"This isn't about our baby."

"I'm sorry, but I don't believe that your feelings could change so abruptly."

"That's the point—it wasn't abrupt at all. I didn't fall in love with you overnight or even during the past four and a half months. I started falling in love with you the first day of Mr. Taylor's eleventh-grade chemistry class—it just took me a while to figure it out."

She wanted to believe him. She really did. But she knew him too well. She knew that he would do anything, say anything, to convince her that he wanted to be with her because he wanted to take responsibility for his child.

And even knowing that, she was tempted to take what he was offering. Because she loved him with her whole heart, and she knew that she always would. But she could still hear the statement that had broken her heart: *the last thing I need is to add a baby to the mix.*

And with those words still echoing in her head, she found the resolve she needed. "I appreciate what you're trying to do, but—"

"What I'm trying to do is prevent you from screwing up both of our lives—and our baby's—because you're too stubborn to believe what I'm telling you."

She lifted her chin. "Forgive me if a declaration of love

doesn't make me want to fall into your arms like a dreamy-eyed heroine at the end of some Hollywood movie."

"Maybe that's the problem. Maybe you've forgotten how to dream."

"I have dreams," she insisted. "But I've learned that plans are much more practical."

"Before you dig your heels in too deep, will you do me a favor?"

"What is it?" she asked warily.

"Come back to Charisma with me—there's something I need to show you."

"I'm here for the weekend with Laurel."

"Please," he said. "Just do this one thing for me. If you want to come back here after, I'll bring you back."

"All right," she finally agreed.

She sent Laurel a text message to let her friend know where she was going. Laurel's reply—give him a chance. I love you but really hope I don't see you again until we're back at school Tuesday—confirmed to Kenna that she was the only one who'd been surprised by Daniel's appearance at the house.

They drove for a while in silence before Daniel said, "Are you feeling okay? Have you had any more morning sickness?"

"I feel fine. Thankfully the nausea only seemed to last a few days."

"Have you seen a doctor?"

"Of course I've seen a doctor."

"Do you know your actual due date?"

"May twenty-second."

He did the mental calculations. "So that morning I came back from Palo Alto?"

She nodded. "I guess the odds were pretty good."

"The things I said that day—"

"The pregnancy was a surprise to both of us," she reminded him. "You don't have to apologize for anything you were thinking or feeling."

"The idea of being a father still terrifies me," he admitted. "But mostly in a good way now."

"Me, too," she admitted.

"You're terrified by the idea that I'm going to be a father?"

The question teased a hint of a smile out of her. "I'm terrified of being a mother," she admitted.

"We can be terrified together."

"If you really do want to be part of our baby's life, I won't stand in your way."

"I am going to be part of our baby's life," he confirmed. "And yours."

She didn't respond to that, because she figured they still had seven months to work out the details and she didn't want to argue with him anymore today.

"Have you told your mother?" he asked.

She shook her head. "I'm not sure I can handle the drama right now."

"How do you think she'll react to the news that she's going to be a grandmother?"

"She already is," she reminded him. "Despite the fact that she's never seen her grandchild."

He'd almost forgotten that Kenna had another sister. She rarely talked about Jayda—maybe because there wasn't much to say about a sibling she hadn't seen in a dozen years. In fact, he'd known Kenna for more than a year before she even mentioned Jayda's name.

He'd taken her to the Sweet Spot after school and bought her a cupcake to celebrate her seventeenth birthday. That was when she'd told him about Jayda's seventeenth birthday, when her sister announced that she was pregnant. Sue Ellen had kicked her out that same night.

So Jayda had moved in with the boyfriend—Daniel couldn't remember his name or even if Kenna had ever mentioned it—and a few months later, the boyfriend had found a job out west so they packed up and moved. Kenna hadn't seen or heard from her sister since; she didn't even know if Jayda had a boy or girl.

"That's one of the reasons I never let myself get involved with anyone in high school," Kenna told him now. "I was terrified that I'd get pregnant by the first guy I slept with." She smiled wryly. "And that's what happened, anyway."

He reached across the console for her hand, linked their fingers together. He took it as a positive sign that she didn't pull away.

Although she'd told him she was over the morning sickness, it seemed that fatigue was still a factor because, within a few minutes, she was asleep. Or maybe, like him, she hadn't been sleeping well, tossing and turning in an empty bed.

She slept the rest of the way back to Charisma, which he didn't mind, because it meant she couldn't see where he was going or speculate on his reasons until they were at their destination.

He pulled into the narrow gravel drive, and she stirred when the vehicle stopped moving.

"We're here," he told her.

He got out of the car and went to open her door.

She looked around at the open space surrounded by trees, uncomprehending. "You wanted to show me a vacant lot?"

"A new beginning," he told her.

She stared at him, still not understanding.

"It's not *my* condo or *your* apartment, it's *ours*."

"Are you telling me that you own this property?"

"*We* own this property—our names are side by side on the title deed. That's what I've been tied up with through most of this past week," he admitted. "Looking for the perfect place to build the home you've always wanted."

That was the problem with marrying a man who knew

all of your hopes and dreams—he could use them to manipulate your emotions.

"Why are you doing this?" she asked him.

"Because I want a home with you, Kenna. A place for us to live together, raise our children together and grow old together."

Not child, but children. As if he wasn't just accepting the baby she already carried but looking to the future, and the sincerity in his tone brought tears to her eyes. But she was still afraid to believe, afraid to let herself hope. Afraid that if she reached for the dream that seemed to be within her grasp, it would simply fade away, as dreams usually did in the light of day.

He framed her face with his hands and looked into her eyes, and she knew that he could see everything she was feeling. But she could see what he was feeling, too, and the depth of emotion in his eyes staggered her.

"Do you remember the day that Ren signed on to drive for GSR?" he asked her now.

Though she was surprised by the apparent shift in topic, she nodded.

"You told me that you were glad I was finally going to have everything I always wanted. And I thought I did," he admitted, still holding her gaze. "When Garrett/Slater Racing became a reality, I thought it was everything I ever wanted.

"Then you walked out on our marriage, and I realized the truth. You're it for me, Kenna. You're everything I ever wanted. And without you, I have absolutely nothing that really matters."

Never in her whole life had anyone ever looked at her the way he was looking at her. Never in her whole life had anyone ever loved her the way Daniel Garrett loved her.

And she knew now that he did. It wasn't just the words he'd spoken. It was the truth of them that shone in his eyes.

And though she tried to hold them back, tears spilled onto her cheeks.

"I'm sorry." He gently brushed the moisture away. "I didn't mean to make you cry. I don't know what else I can do.... I just needed you to know how I feel. This isn't about our baby or doing the right thing—except if the right thing is the two of us together. Because that's what I really want, Kenna. I want you by my side, not just for the next eight months but forever."

"I want that, too," she finally admitted.

He breathed out a sigh and rested his forehead against hers. "Tell me you love me."

"I love you, Daniel." She looked up at him. "That sounds so inadequate after everything you just said."

"It sounds perfect," he assured her.

And then, finally, he kissed her.

"Now I feel like a dreamy-eyed heroine at the end of a Hollywood movie," she told him.

"Except this isn't our ending—it's only our beginning."

Epilogue

They renewed their vows on New Year's Eve in front of a small gathering of their family and closest friends. And this time, when the minister told the groom to kiss his bride, there was absolutely no hesitation. It was a new year and a new beginning, and they were eager to embrace both.

They moved into their new home—a two-story design of brick and stone with five bedrooms, four baths and dozens of windows to let in natural light—the first weekend in May, less than two weeks before Kenna's due date. The Garrett family turned out en masse to help, and even Sue Ellen and Becca stopped by. Daniel had turned into a typically overprotective expectant father and he refused to let Kenna do anything. He didn't even let her unpack dishes in the kitchen, but willingly performed the task under her direction and supervision.

After everyone had gone, they ate pizza and drank non-alcoholic champagne and then he made love to her, slowly and sweetly, in their new bed in their new home.

She was hugely pregnant, but Daniel didn't care. In fact,

he seemed to love touching her and insisted that she'd never been more beautiful. She suspected that his fascination was mostly centered on her bigger breasts, but she didn't mind.

Two weeks later, two days *after* Kenna's due date, their baby had still given no indication that he or she was ready to be born. Kenna was anxious and frustrated and annoyed by Daniel's hovering. For the past several weeks, he'd insisted on staying close to home—just in case. But the race this weekend was in Concord, barely more than a two-hour drive away, so she practically shoved him out the door.

Of course, he still refused to leave her alone and called his mother to stay with her until he got back. Kenna didn't object to that—she enjoyed Jane's company. And she felt reassured by the presence of a woman who had been through the whole pregnancy and labor experience—three times.

As Kenna closed her eyes to breathe through another contraction—because, of course, her labor had started just after Daniel had called to confirm his arrival at the racetrack—she was beginning to have doubts that she would get through this labor, never mind want to do it again.

On Jane's advice, she'd already had a long soak in the jetted tub of their master bath, which had been heavenly, and now she was seated in front of the television with a heating pad against her lower back.

The green-and-gold number seven-twenty-two car driven by Ren D'Alesio was running in second place, as it had through most of the two hundred and thirty laps that had been completed so far. After crashing midway through the inaugural race of the season, he'd started to have some modest success. Working with his team, he'd learned to temper his aggressiveness with patience, and it had paid off with two top-ten finishes in recent weeks.

He was still looking for his first win, and although she knew a lot of drivers raced for years without getting one, she couldn't help feeling that he was close. Or maybe she just really wanted the win—for Ren and GSR and especially for Daniel, because she knew how hard he'd worked to get the team to where it was at now.

And right now, she really wanted their baby to hold off being born until the race was done and his or her daddy got home, but she was beginning to have serious doubts that would happen.

"Fifteen minutes," Jane said, announcing the time since Kenna's last contraction. "I really think we should go to the hospital now."

"After I see the number seven-twenty-two car cross the finish line," Kenna bargained.

"You can see it on the sports channel highlights," her mother-in-law assured her.

"But I promised Daniel that I'd watch the race."

"You also promised that you'd call if there was any indication that you were in labor," her husband said from the doorway.

She spun around, surprised and thrilled, to see him. "What are you doing here? You're supposed to be in Concord!"

"I'm here because someone—and it wasn't my wife— called to tell me that my wife was in labor."

"Early stages of labor," Kenna said, fingers crossed.

"I think I'd be more willing to believe that if I heard it from a doctor," Daniel told her.

"But Ren's going to win this one—I can feel it."

"I'd be happy with a top-five finish *and* with you at the hospital," her husband said.

"There's only another one hundred and sixty-eight laps to—" She sucked in a breath as another contraction tightened her belly.

"We're going *now*," Daniel told her.

It took Lorenzo D'Alesio four hours, twenty-six minutes and fifty-three seconds to complete the four hundred laps at Charlotte Motor Speedway and take the checkered flag. It took Kenna almost as long to push an eight-pound thirteen-ounce baby into the world.

Of course, she did her job without a pit crew at her beck and call, although she did have most of the Garrett family popping in and out of her room periodically to offer encouragement and check on her progress. And she had a husband who never left her side for a single minute during that intense period of labor.

And when their naked and squalling baby boy was transferred to his hands for the first time, she watched the array of emotions that crossed over his face. Joy. Terror. Pride. Relief. And, most of all, love.

When he finally lifted his gaze to hers, the tears in his eyes matched her own.

After the baby had been weighed and measured and returned to his happy but exhausted parents, the room began to fill with visitors. Most of Daniel's immediate family were there, and a few cousins stopped by, as well as Sue Ellen and Becca.

"Does he have a name?" Becca wanted to know.

Daniel looked at Kenna, and she nodded.

"Jacob Scott Garrett."

"Jacob...after your grandfather?" Jane asked.

"It seemed appropriate," Daniel said, and smiled at his wife. "Since, in a roundabout way, he got us to where we are today."

When the baby started to fuss, Daniel shooed everyone out so that Kenna could nurse their son and they could all get some rest.

Nate was the last to leave, and paused in the doorway on his way out. "Oh—in case you haven't heard, he won."

Daniel looked at him blankly.

"Ren D'Alesio," his brother clarified. "Driving the number seven-twenty-two car for Garrett/Slater Racing. He made his move on the second turn of the last lap and never looked back."

"I knew it," Kenna said as Nate walked out. Then she looked at her husband in silent apology. "And you missed it."

"Ren's going to win a lot of races." He sat down beside the bed and took her hand, linking their fingers together. "The birth of our first child—that was a once-in-a-lifetime experience and one that I wouldn't have missed for anything in the world."

"You're really not disappointed that you weren't there?"

"I am exactly where I want to be," he assured her. "For now and forever."

* * * * *

Don't miss Nate Garrett's story,
the next installment in award-winning author
Brenda Harlen's Special Edition miniseries
THOSE ENGAGING GARRETTS!
Coming in 2015, wherever Harlequin books are sold.

COMING NEXT MONTH FROM

H HARLEQUIN®

SPECIAL EDITION

Available August 19, 2014

#2353 MAVERICK FOR HIRE
Montana Mavericks: 20 Years in the Saddle! • by Leanne Banks
Nick Pritchett has a love 'em and leave 'em attitude...except when it comes to his best friend, Cecelia Clifton. When the pretty brunette insists on finding a beau, the hunky carpenter realizes that he can't lose Cecelia to another man. Nick may be Mr. Fix-It in Rust Creek Falls, but his BFF has done a number on his heart!

#2354 WEARING THE RANCHER'S RING
Men of the West • by Stella Bagwell
Cowboy Clancy Calhoun always had room for only one woman in his heart—his ex-fiancée, Olivia Parsons, who left him years ago. So when Olivia returns home to Nevada for work, Clancy is blown away. But can the handsome rancher simultaneously heal his wounded heart *and* convince Olivia to start a life together at long last?

#2355 A MATCH MADE BY BABY
The Mommy Club • by Karen Rose Smith
Adam Preston never worried about babies...until he had his sister's infant to care for! Bewildered at his new responsibilities, Adam asks pediatrician Kaitlyn Foster for help. The good doctor is reluctant to give her assistance, but once she does, she just can't resist the bachelor and his adorable niece.

#2356 NOT JUST A COWBOY
Texas Rescue • by Caro Carson
Texan oil heiress Patricia Cargill is particular when it comes to her men, but there's just something about Luke Waterson she can't resist. Maybe it's that he's a drop-dead gorgeous rescue fireman and ranch hand! Luke, who lights long-dormant fires in Patricia, has also got his fair share of secrets. Can the cowboy charm the socialite into a happily-ever-after?

#2357 ONCE UPON A BRIDE
by Helen Lacey
Although she owns a bridal shop, Lauren Jakowski can't imagine herself taking the trip down the aisle anytime soon. In fact, she's sworn off men for the foreseeable future! But Cupid intervenes in the form of her new next-door neighbor, Gabe Vitali. Despite his tragic past, the cancer survivor might just be the key to Lauren's future.

#2358 HIS TEXAS FOREVER FAMILY
by Amy Woods
After a difficult divorce, art teacher Liam Campbell wants nothing more than to start anew in Peach Leaf, Texas. He's instantly captivated by his new boss, Paige Graham, but the lovely widow has placed romance on the back burner to care for her emotionally wounded young son and focus on her career. Still, as Liam bonds with the boy and his mother, a new family begins to blossom.

YOU CAN FIND MORE INFORMATION ON UPCOMING HARLEQUIN® TITLES, FREE EXCERPTS AND MORE AT WWW.HARLEQUIN.COM.

HSECNM0814

REQUEST YOUR FREE BOOKS!

2 FREE NOVELS PLUS 2 FREE GIFTS!

⊕HARLEQUIN

SPECIAL EDITION

Life, Love & Family

YES! Please send me 2 FREE Harlequin® Special Edition novels and my 2 FREE gifts (gifts are worth about $10). After receiving them, if I don't wish to receive any more books, I can return the shipping statement marked "cancel." If I don't cancel, I will receive 6 brand-new novels every month and be billed just $4.74 per book in the U.S. or $5.24 per book in Canada. That's a savings of at least 14% off the cover price! It's quite a bargain! Shipping and handling is just 50¢ per book in the U.S. and 75¢ per book in Canada.* I understand that accepting the 2 free books and gifts places me under no obligation to buy anything. I can always return a shipment and cancel at any time. Even if I never buy another book, the two free books and gifts are mine to keep forever.

235/335 HDN F45Y

Name	(PLEASE PRINT)

Address		Apt. #

City	State/Prov.	Zip/Postal Code

Signature (if under 18, a parent or guardian must sign)

Mail to the **Harlequin®** Reader Service:
IN U.S.A.: P.O. Box 1867, Buffalo, NY 14240-1867
IN CANADA: P.O. Box 609, Fort Erie, Ontario L2A 5X3

Want to try two free books from another line?
Call 1-800-873-8635 or visit www.ReaderService.com.

* Terms and prices subject to change without notice. Prices do not include applicable taxes. Sales tax applicable in N.Y. Canadian residents will be charged applicable taxes. Offer not valid in Quebec. This offer is limited to one order per household. Not valid for current subscribers to Harlequin Special Edition books. All orders subject to credit approval. Credit or debit balances in a customer's account(s) may be offset by any other outstanding balance owed by or to the customer. Please allow 4 to 6 weeks for delivery. Offer available while quantities last.

Your Privacy—The Harlequin® Reader Service is committed to protecting your privacy. Our Privacy Policy is available online at www.ReaderService.com or upon request from the Harlequin Reader Service.

We make a portion of our mailing list available to reputable third parties that offer products we believe may interest you. If you prefer that we not exchange your name with third parties, or if you wish to clarify or modify your communication preferences, please visit us at www.ReaderService.com/consumerschoice or write to us at Harlequin Reader Service Preference Service, P.O. Box 9062, Buffalo, NY 14269. Include your complete name and address.